Suzanna Keating –

She's twenty-seven, single and beautiful—inside *and* out. She's still reeling from the blow life dealt her three months ago: the deaths of her beloved sister and brother-in-law. Her only consolation is Timmy, her four-year-old nephew. For Timmy's sake, she's had to pull herself together and get on with living. Now he's the center of her universe.

Logan Bradford

As old-money and blue-blooded as a New Englander can get. The death, three months ago, of his estranged younger brother, Harris, has hit him hard, and now he has this guardianship issue to contend with. It's obviously not going to be the uncontested move he and his father had envisioned. But despite his falling-out with Harris, he feels a very real responsibility toward the boy.

Timmy Bradford

He loves hot dogs, his new puppy, Buddy, and his pretty Auntie Sue. He doesn't love his Uncle Logan and his grandfather. Why should he? He's never even *met* them. That's why it's so scary when he has to go and live with them. But maybe...if his uncle marries his aunt...he'll have a *real* family!

NY

Dear Reader,

Raising children is never easy, and my husband and I certainly had our share of difficulties raising ours. There were the standard emergency-room runs, the school plays gone awry and, later, conversations that started, "You've been diving off *which* bridge?" But there's one day that stands out in my mind as the indisputable worst. It was the day I discovered my seven-year-old daughter and two of her friends were missing. Gone. As in lost in the woods. Or maybe abducted. It surely looked that way when I found their bikes strewn on the side of a wooded dead-end road.

It was the weekend, so all parents were home. We gathered quickly and began making forays into the woods. Soon we were joined by neighbors, reporters, thirty firemen and police, and a team of tracking dogs.

I'll spare you the details of our agony that day and merely say that in the end the girls were found—not by bloodhounds but by my husband. Tired but safe, they were walking home from an amusement park *five miles away*, which they'd simply taken a notion to visit! They'd gone through the woods because none of them was allowed to walk on the highway.

Despite the difficulties, I thoroughly enjoyed raising my children. In fact, I had the time of my life and would gladly do it all again (*if* I was also guaranteed the same energy level I had twenty years ago). I really believe children are life's greatest joy. My son and daughter are now grown, yet never a day goes by that they don't add a depth and richness to my life that wouldn't be there without them.

Therefore, I'm thrilled to be leading off this new Harlequin Romance promotion celebrating children. I hope you enjoy reading *The Baby Battle* as much as I enjoyed writing it.

Sincerely,

Shannon Waverly

THE BABY BATTLE
Shannon Waverly

Harlequin Books

TORONTO • NEW YORK • LONDON
AMSTERDAM • PARIS • SYDNEY • HAMBURG
STOCKHOLM • ATHENS • TOKYO • MILAN
MADRID • WARSAW • BUDAPEST • AUCKLAND

To Christopher and Jessica—
Love always,
Mom

ISBN 0-373-03316-8

THE BABY BATTLE

Copyright © 1994 by Kathleen Shannon.

This edition published by arrangement with Harlequin Enterprises B. V.

® and TM are trademarks of the publisher. Trademarks indicated with ® are registered in the United States Patent and Trademark Office, the Canadian Trade Marks Office and in other countries.

Printed in U.S.A.

CHAPTER ONE

SHE COULD HANDLE this. She could. All she had to do was take a deep breath and regain her sense of perspective. After all, it was only a few dozen shower favors, right? No one had died. The earth was still spinning.

Suzanna snatched up the squirming dog, shut him in the washroom at the back of the shop, then returned to the narrow storage room where her nephew still sat amid the lacy debris, an incriminating dribble of chocolate running down his chin.

"And what do you have to say for yourself, young man?" Hands on her hips, Suzanna glared at the child as sternly as she could.

"I'm sorry, Auntie Sue." At four years old, Timmy could sometimes be more than a handful.

"How many times have I told you to stay out of this room, especially now that we have a puppy? These favors take a lot of time to make, time I don't have. The party I'm catering is tomorrow."

Timmy's big blue eyes filled with tears, which very nearly broke Suzanna's heart. Of all the parenting duties she'd had to assume since the accident three months ago, discipline was the hardest.

She got down on one knee and gripped his tiny shoulders. "Okay, I know you'll watch Buddy more carefully from now on and this won't ever happen again. Right?"

The child nodded, his lower lip quivering.

"Good. Now pick up all this mess and put it in that basket. I've got to go write out Marie's paycheck, and then..." Suzanna checked her watch and felt a pang of guilt. No wonder he'd gone foraging. "Then we'll have our lunch."

The crisis over, Timmy sighed in trembling relief, and Suzanna couldn't help hugging him. She kissed his cheek, his silky brown hair, and then his other cheek. Only when he began to wiggle did she realize how tightly she was squeezing.

"Sorry, love." Smiling, she got to her feet just as the phone in her office rang. "Augh! What now?" she called, laughter in her voice even though she *was* beginning to feel genuinely frazzled. First, the pipe leak on the third floor, then the meat delivery coming two hours late. After that she'd gone a round with the mother of the bride-to-be who didn't understand why half of tomorrow's shower menu couldn't be changed. And now she was going to be up till who knew when remaking those fussy little favors.

"Please, can you answer?" Marie called back. Marie was one of two part-time helpers Suzanna employed. "I'm up to my elbows in pie crust."

"Sure enough. And, Tim, don't forget—pick up everything." Suzanna hurried across the hall to her office, which was really just a thinly partitioned space similar to the windowless storage room, except that this room contained a derelict desk. Wincing against the yipping of the jailed dog, she yanked the receiver from its hook and said, "Fiesta Catering."

"Suzanna Keating, please." It was a man's voice, one she didn't recognize.

"Speaking." Tucking the phone between her ear and shoulder, she began to shuffle the clutter on her desk.

"This is Logan Bradford, Miss Keating."

She was flipping through a stack of mail when the name registered. The envelopes slipped from her grasp. "I b-beg your pardon?"

"Logan Bradford. Harris's brother. We met briefly at the funeral."

Suzanna sank into her office chair, her legs suddenly too weak to keep her standing. "Yes. Um . . . what?"

"I'd like to speak with you if I may. I'm in the city right now on business and could meet you at your place."

Suzanna straightened, adrenaline fizzing through her nervous system. "Mr. Bradford, I can't imagine anything we have to say to each other."

"On the contrary, we have a great deal to say." He spoke with a tone and phrasing that Suzanna could only classify as aristocratic. But then, he was. As old-money and blue-blooded as a New Englander could get.

"I'm sorry I haven't called since the funeral," he continued, sounding not the least bit sorry. "I thought we all needed a few months to be alone with our grief. But the time for a talk has definitely arrived, and I really prefer to speak with you in person. This isn't the sort of thing one discusses on the phone."

Suzanna clutched the top of her head. "I—I'm sorry, I'm extremely busy today and—"

"It won't take long. I'm in my car at the moment. In fact, I'm only two blocks from you."

Suzanna gulped. She'd never heard a voice so determined to have its way. "But—"

"It's important, Miss Keating. I'll see you in a couple of minutes."

The line went dead, leaving Suzanna gaping into space. She couldn't think a single coherent thought, aware only of the pounding of her heart. Slowly she returned the receiver to its cradle.

Logan Bradford was coming *here?* She got to her feet, wiped her damp palms down the sides of her flour-dusted apron and checked her reflection in the small frameless mirror by the door. The day was hot and muggy, even for August, and her flushed face wore a sheen of perspiration.

She hadn't bothered with makeup this morning and had simply secured her long dark hair in a hasty braid. Under her apron she was wearing a plain white T-shirt and loose-fitting blue cotton shorts, an outfit chosen for comfort rather than style.

Abruptly she swung from the mirror, abashed to realize she'd been standing there concerned about her appearance. What in heaven's name was the matter with her? Harris's brother was on his way over, the same brother who'd refused to give him any sort of support when their father cast him out of their house five years ago, the same brother who, even worse, had sided with that odious old man and agreed that to marry anyone as lowly as Suzanna's sister was a sin worthy of disinheritance. Logan Bradford was coming by for a "talk," and she hadn't the foggiest notion why. Nor did she know how she was going to get through that talk without unleashing the anger she'd harbored toward him and his father for nearly five years.

Was he finally coming by to collect his brother's belongings? Did he actually think Harris had left anything of value? Precious family heirlooms perhaps?

Suzanna's breathing came hard and fast. Harris had owned nothing five years ago except what he'd had in his dorm room, and pride had kept him from going back to the house for anything else. He did have his stereo, but he'd sold that, sold his watch and leather jacket, too, before Suzanna assured him she would help. Even though she hadn't been all that happy about the marriage herself, he was still her little sister's husband and so of course she'd help. Wasn't that what family was for?

Timmy shuffled out of the storage room then, dragging the basket of chewed-up lace and ribbon.

"Thanks, love." At the sight of him, Suzanna's heart contracted. Life had been inordinately cruel to this little nephew of hers, a car accident taking both his parents in one brutal afternoon. Sometimes Suzanna still couldn't believe they were gone, still found herself listening for their laughter on the stairs. And the pain she suffered when she remembered she was never going to see them again—sometimes it was almost too much to bear. At times like those she could only wonder what Timmy was going through.

If there was any consolation to be found, it was in the fact that Suzanna had always been close to her nephew. Living in the same house, she hadn't been just an aunt; she'd been virtually a third parent from the day he was born. She hoped that fact was making the transition a little less traumatic for him.

He was certainly making the past few months easier for her. Losing Claudia and Harris had been the worst experience of her life, but for Timmy's sake she'd had to pull herself together right after the funeral and get on with living. Now he was the center of her universe, concern for his welfare and future the fuel that propelled her through her day. She hadn't realized how the addition of a child could give one's life such clear definition and purpose.

She took the basket, set it on her desk and led Timmy out front. Marie, a blocky sixty-year-old widow, was busily rolling crust for tomorrow's quiches on a marble-topped counter in the center of the shop, the same counter Suzanna's parents had rolled pastry on for nearly thirty years. Along the right wall, the long glass-doored coolers hummed to their contents of salad and cold cuts, while the mouth-watering aroma of *chourico* sausage and peppers, simmering on a stainless steel stove, spiced the air. Two newly barred plate-glass windows faced the street.

This had been Suzanna's world all twenty-seven years of her life—this shop, this street, this southeastern Massachusetts mill town whose boom and glory had long ago faded with the migration of the textile industry south. And while most of the friends she'd grown up with had run off to the suburbs, she had remained, as stalwart as the monolithic granite mills that surrounded her.

"Marie, could you give Timmy his lunch today? I'm expecting a visitor in a few minutes."

Marie wiped her hands on a wet towel. "Come on, young man. Let's see what we've got in the cooler. Are you in the mood for lobster salad today?"

"Hot dogs," he answered, excitement building in his voice.

"Hot dogs. I offer the man lobster and he wants hot dogs." Marie shook her head, laughing.

Watching Timmy skip off, Suzanna smiled cautiously. The boy seemed to be doing well these days, better than she'd expected. After two months of regressive behavior, he was no longer wetting his bed, and his spells of fretfulness and whining occurred so infrequently they were probably the norm for someone his age. Still, Suzanna watched over him vigilantly. And worried.

Seeing he was occupied, she hurried through the shop and up the back stairs to their first-floor apartment. Suzanna's catering business was technically located in the basement, but because the house was set into a hill, the front of the basement opened directly onto the sidewalk. This feature made it ideal for commerce, and, in fact, it had been used as a store even in the 1920s when the sturdy three-decker was built.

Suzanna had only enough time to remove her apron before she heard an automobile pulling over to the curb. She opened the kitchen door and stepped out to the entryway, which always seemed to hold the faint mingled smells of whatever she and her tenants had cooked the evening before. But the air sifting through the warped screening of the outer door was hardly better. It smelled of car exhaust and the river, and was thick with noise: children, grown bored and petulant with summer, squabbling; air brakes from trash trucks belching; fire engines; rap music; church bells chiming the Angelus.

Suzanna pulled in a lungful of this tired August air and forced herself to peer down the walk. Below the short flight of granite steps that led up to her yard from the sidewalk idled a long black limousine. She swallowed and felt a shiver race down her spine. *Something is terribly wrong with this moment,* she thought, experiencing a sudden urge to close and bolt the door.

But she didn't. The engine stilled and the man she remembered as Logan Bradford emerged from the car. Standing on the sidewalk, he squared his broad shoulders, buttoned his suit jacket and gave her property a slow squint-eyed appraisal.

Suzanna bristled. She was well aware that what he was looking at was a far cry from the Bradford estate out on Mattashaum Harbor, but it wasn't a slum, either. And given the cold unfeeling atmosphere of Mattashaum, his younger brother had been more than willing to call this vibrant ethnic neighborhood his home.

Logan Bradford's critical gaze traveled up the street to businesses much like her own: a small convenience store, a family-run fish market, a florist. It noted laundry sagging from back-window lines and yards crowded with vegetable gardens and grape arbors whose fruit would be used to make wine. It took in street-facing windows that showcased arrangements of bright plastic flowers and plaster saints, took in the men's athletic club that was, in reality, just a barroom, and with a turn, the smokestacks from the mills farther down the hill, mills in which her ancestors had toiled and his had owned. The more he observed, the straighter she stood.

And then he spotted her, standing at the screen door of her side entry with her arms tightly crossed, and the neighborhood lost interest for him. With a dismissive hitch of his shoulders, he started for the steps.

"Oh, Lord," Suzanna whispered, pressing a hand to her panicking stomach.

He seemed taller than she remembered and definitely more intimidating. Everything about him today bespoke money and power, from the cut of his impeccable dark suit to the uncompromising set of his handsome face. He walked with purpose, back straight, gaze unflinching, and for a moment Suzanna suffered the light-headed dizziness she'd experienced the first time they met.

She didn't think he remembered that night. Their first encounter hadn't been the funeral but a party she'd catered two years before.

For the most part, she did affairs within the city, but two years ago, to increase business, she'd decided to place an ad in the suburban newspapers, and someone from one of the outlying towns had hired her to do a cocktail party.

"You realize where that is, don't you?" Harris had laughed.

She'd shrugged, unable to peg the exact location.

"Double your prices, sweetheart. That's all I'm gonna say."

Her new client's home had turned out to be an immense Victorian summer cottage located on one of the exclusive points south of the city along the Atlantic coast. Suzanna was nervous but excited. Finally, a chance to stretch her culinary talents and charge a fee commensurate with her labor! She enlisted Marie's help, made sure they wore similar black dresses to appear in uniform and drove to the beachfront house with her van filled with hors d'oeuvres fit for a royal gala.

She did well that evening. Several guests even asked for her card. But then *he* walked into the party, Logan Bradford, although at the time she didn't know who he was. With their families entrenched more deeply in their different worlds than the Montagues and Capulets, they had never met.

Not that she hadn't wanted to. After the financial hardships and emotional pain he and his father had caused Harris and Claudia, she had wanted to march down to Mattashaum and duke it out herself. In fact, only Harris's impassioned plea had kept her from going.

She was carrying a tray of blini with caviar into the dining room when she noticed him. He was standing in the adjacent parlor talking to a small circle of people. As he spoke, his gaze lifted and met hers and casually lowered again— then ricocheted right back, alert, almost startled. His reaction was one of the few genuine double takes Suzanna had ever witnessed, and it stopped her dead in her tracks.

Did any details really register in that moment? What he was wearing? The color of his eyes or the cut of his hair? Suzanna didn't think so. All she knew was a sensation of awareness, an awareness so acute, so thrilling and yet so painful that she literally grew faint.

How long the moment lasted she didn't know, but at some point a short blonde standing beside Logan touched his arm, eye contact broke, and after a pause and a slight shake of his head, he continued his conversation.

Suzanna set down her tray and proceeded to gather up used plates and glasses. But the evening had changed for her. Her head was swimming and her leg muscles trembled. She truly feared she wouldn't be able to function the rest of the evening.

As it turned out, she very nearly couldn't. Whenever they were together in the same room, she was overcome by a curiosity so intense it sent her tripping over thresholds and bumping into chairs.

Like most of the other guests, he was casually dressed, wearing a faded brown shirt rolled at the sleeves, pleated tan trousers and scuffed topsiders. Although it was October, he was deeply tanned, with a slash of fresh windburn accenting his high cheekbones, and his straight brown hair still shone with streaks of summer sun. To Suzanna everything about him that night seemed warm and earthy.

"Marie," she'd called in a loud whisper, peeking through the louvers of the kitchen door. "What do you think of that one there?" They'd been commenting on guests all night to help pass the time.

Marie pressed close. "Which?"

"The gorgeous one, six two, six three, with the long British-type face and sleepy bedroom eyes."

"*Which?*"

"Longish hair. Stubborn jaw. Intelligent brow. No, over by the china cabinet."

"Ahh." The older woman smiled knowingly. "Nice." She drew the word out.

"Yes, definitely nice."

Several moments passed while they continued to study their subject. In Suzanna's estimation, he dominated the room with his powerful build and formidable good looks. But there was something beyond the physical that set him apart. Something in the eyes, those deep crystalline gray eyes with the deceptively sleepy lids. They seemed to burn with a fire from within.

"You know," Marie finally said, "he even looks rich." She shook her head, puzzled. "How do they do that? I mean, he needs a haircut. His clothes are nothing special...."

Suzanna might have mentioned that his shirt alone had probably cost more than Marie's entire outfit, but she didn't. "I told you, Marie, it's his attitude. There stands a man who owes the world absolutely nothing." Through the slats she watched him take a sip of his drink, turn, speak, smile, everything about him self-assured and self-contained.

"So, are you gonna make a play for him?" Marie asked drolly. "Or is this one mine?" They both fell to giggling before resuming their work.

Suzanna was glad they'd taken a moment to make light of the situation because, quite frankly, it was making her nervous. A few times when she'd happened to glance his way, she'd found him looking back, and she was beginning to get the feeling he just might approach her before the night was out.

But during one of her subsequent trips through the living room to collect empty serving trays, she heard the blonde who'd apparently come as his date call to him across the room. Logan, she called him. Logan, honey, to be precise.

For the second time that evening, Suzanna felt thunderstruck, but this time there was nothing at all pleasurable about the experience.

Logan? That name wasn't exactly a common one. And given the location of the party, given the guests...

With pounding heart, she took a closer look. But of course. His eyes were the same pale blue-gray, his eyebrows slanted in the same bold line, and his chin—there was the same slight cleft. Why hadn't she noticed the resemblance sooner?

She'd ducked into the kitchen and tried to calm her racing heart. But even now, two and a half years later, the experience still had the power to make her cringe with humiliation. All those interested glances, all that speculation—over Harris's brother?

She'd stayed in the kitchen as long as she could, but finally had no choice but to venture out. However, she soon realized she had nothing to dread. Logan Bradford never looked at her again. The curiosity was gone, the interest spent—or maybe it had never been there to begin with except in her imagination. After all, she was merely a caterer while he was a multimillionaire. Before long he said goodnight to the hostess, took his blonde by the elbow and left the party.

Suzanna didn't see him again until the funeral. Apparently enough time had passed to thoroughly wipe that evening—and her—from his memory. Which was fine. It would've been too embarrassing if he did remember.

The funeral.

Suzanna didn't call Mattashaum herself to deliver the news of the accident. She'd waited until all the arrangements were made and then asked the funeral director to phone. The Bradfords needed to know that Harris had died, but she certainly didn't have to share her grief with them. After the heartless way they'd treated Harris and Claudia, they had relinquished the right.

Logan showed up at the church alone and had the good grace not to sit with her family. He went to the cemetery, too, although, while the rest of the mourners huddled under a canopy, he stood apart in the cold May drizzle. Suzanna didn't care. She disdained everything he stood for, money and power, prejudice and elitism, and wished she could tell him to leave. But of course she couldn't. Couldn't do anything but glare at him occasionally as he stood beneath a thinly budded oak, hands in the pockets of his trench coat, his polished black shoes getting as damp as his hair.

He waited until everyone but Suzanna had left. Only then did he approach the graveside and introduce himself. His composure astounded her. She had been crying for three days and still couldn't stop.

"I'm sorry for the loss of your sister," he said, staring rather indifferently, she thought, at the two flower-draped coffins awaiting burial.

She nodded, reluctant to acknowledge his condolence.

"Where is their son?"

"Back..." She stopped to blow her nose. "Back at the house with a baby-sitter."

"Ah." He nodded, not really interested. "I hope you don't mind my being here."

She thought about the impropriety of arguing at that particular time, but her pain was too deep for her to remain silent. "I'd mind it less if you'd visited them when it mattered."

He lifted his chiseled chin and tightened his mouth. "My brother made his choices. He had to live with the consequences."

Suzanna turned her head and stared up at him in amazed disdain. She'd never heard anything so hard-hearted in her life. "Bravo, Mr. Bradford. Not a note of doubt or regret right to the end."

The look he cast her was withering.

She cast it right back. "Why did you even bother to come?"

He was quiet awhile, his gaze unfocused. "We have a family plot out at Mattashaum," he finally answered. "My father would like the body moved there."

"The body?" His word choice dried her tears and galvanized her anger. "Can't you even say your brother's name in death? Good Lord! I've heard of pride, but this is sick." She shook her head, hoping he knew how little she thought of him. "I'm sorry, Mr. Bradford. Harris stays right here with my sister. It's where he belongs now."

Logan lifted his steely eyes to the scudding gray clouds, and his jaw set even harder. "We'll see," he replied.

Suzanna tried to think of something clever and hurtful to throw back at him, but before she could, he flipped up his coat collar and stepped out into the drizzle.

But just as he was passing his brother's coffin, he paused a moment. Paused with his aloof gaze moving over the greening cemetery. Paused as if he was merely caught within an idle thought—were his car keys in the ignition? Or where would he stop for lunch?

Suzanna watched, more curious than hateful. And then almost imperceptibly his hand began to lift. Even as Logan's eyes roamed the horizon, he lifted his hand and pressed it to the rain-sleeked wood—gently, the way someone might touch the head of a slumbering child. "Godspeed, Harry," he whispered. Then, pulling in a breath that lifted his strong shoulders, he'd strode off to his waiting car....

And now that same man was mounting her granite stairs, treading up her walk, climbing her creaking porch steps. And as he climbed, the thought crossed her mind that perhaps he was here to discuss moving Harris's body. She lifted her head, more resolved than ever to thwart him.

Under the porch overhang he paused, watching her from the other side of the screen door. His eyes were as gray as winter ice, his mouth just as hard, and unexpectedly her thoughts turned back to the party more than two years earlier when, for a few unguarded hours, she had found him so warm and captivating. She shuddered, realizing how foolish her instincts could be.

"What's this all about?" she asked without ceremony.

"May I come in?"

Suzanna had been raised to be impeccably polite, but now she shook her head. "If your business with me is as brief as you claim, we can conduct it right here."

"Fine," he said crisply. He unbuttoned his jacket, the same jacket he'd just buttoned out on the sidewalk, brushed it open and fit his hands into his pants pockets. "I've come to talk about my brother's child."

Suzanna's head jerked back. "Timmy?"

"Yes."

"Timmy?" she repeated, nonplussed. When he only stared at her, she added, "What about?"

"Now that Harris is gone, I intend to assume guardianship of the boy." His eyes never swerved from hers. They didn't even blink. In fact, he spoke with such quiet certitude that it was a few seconds before his meaning registered.

"You're what?" She laughed, sure he was joking.

"Despite our falling-out with Harris, my father and I feel a very real responsibility toward his son. He is a Bradford, after all."

Such anger surged through Suzanna she felt dizzy with it. "Oh, I see. *Now* he's a Bradford. Now, when it's too late to do anyone any real good."

One dark eyebrow arched in an incredulous curve. "On the contrary, coming home can do the boy nothing but good." His gaze lifted and swept the neighborhood, his meaning clear.

"Wait just a second." Suzanna swung the aluminum door open so forcefully it bashed against his leg. The corner of his mouth hardened as he stepped back. "Timmy has a home right here with me. What makes you think I'd let him go off with you?"

Logan Bradford stared down his straight imperious nose at her. "And what makes you think you have any say in the matter?"

She laughed again, but the sound was high and tight with nervousness. "Well, who do you suppose has been caring for him since his parents died?"

"True, but as far as I can see, neither Harris nor your sister left a will naming you legal guardian. Did they?"

"Well, no. They were so young the thought never crossed their minds, but—"

"In which case I, as the boy's uncle, am ready to assume guardianship."

Suzanna squinched her eyes tight. "We're not communicating, are we? You see, I'm Timmy's guardian. Me." She pressed her fingertips to her chest as if he needed a visual aid.

"Not legally," he said evenly. "Look, I came here hoping we could be reasonable about this and not turn it into another—"

"Reasonable? Are you trying to say that shipping a recently orphaned four-year-old to a strange house full of strange people is reasonable?"

"Yes," he answered without hesitation. "We may be strangers now, but he's young—he'll adjust quickly. And once he does, he'll have every advantage a Bradford is heir to. I should think you'd be happy about that prospect."

Suzanna suddenly realized he believed every word he was saying. She passed a shaky hand over her forehead. "This...this doesn't make sense. You people didn't acknowledge his birth, you cared nothing about his welfare for four years, and suddenly you want to become his guardian and expect me to be happy about it?" Her voice wobbled more precariously by the second. "Mr. Bradford, you'd better get off my property right now before I call the police."

She saw anger flash in his crystal-gray eyes, yet when he spoke, he exhibited a great deal of control. "All right, enough," he said, raising a placating hand. But instead of leaving, he sat back against the porch rail and for a long while studied her, one index finger curved over his lips in a pensive cautious pose. Under his scrutiny, Suzanna began to feel like a specimen being dissected.

"All right," he said again, this time resolutely. He unfolded his arms and stood away from the rail. "My father and I appreciate the time and effort you've invested in Harris's son these past few months, and we'll be happy to compensate you, say...twenty thousand dollars?"

Suzanna stared at him in disbelief. "You want to *pay* me for taking care of Timmy?"

"That's right. Provided you agree to let me care for him from now on."

Outrage overwhelmed her. "You big condescending jerk!" Her hands clenched into fists at her sides. "What kind of lowlife do you think I am?"

"Twenty-five thousand," Logan returned, unruffled.

"Ugh!" She threw up her hands in disgust.

"Thirty thousand's my last offer. I won't go any higher."

"You people think money's the answer to everything, don't you?"

His dark head tilted, his eyes cutting through her again, reassessing. "Okay, how about you telling *me* how much you wa— How much your time is worth."

"This isn't about money, Mr. Bradford. It's about love, something you obviously don't know the first thing about. Jeez, didn't you people learn anything after trying to buy off my sister?"

Suzanna saw him blink—and wondered if she'd struck a raw nerve.

Looking aside, Logan pushed his hand through his hair, fingers splayed. When he looked at her again, whatever composure she'd shaken was back in place. "This has always been about money, Miss Keating. From the day your sister and Harris first met."

"What are you talking about?"

He smiled coldly. "Do you actually think that if your sister hadn't trapped my brother with her pregnancy, they would have stayed together?"

She gasped. "You think Claudia got pregnant on purpose?"

"I know she did. It's a very common, very reliable ploy. Harry would've left her years ago otherwise."

"You can't still believe she was after his money!"

"Somebody sure as hell was." He pinned her with a sharp, accusing stare.

"Me? You're accusing *me* of being after Harris's money?"

His mouth curled in answer.

"But Harris didn't have any money."

"I know, and he wasn't going to come into any, either, as long as he continued to act so immaturely. But I can understand how an outsider might think he would. And if that outsider had spent five years supporting him, it wouldn't be unreasonable for her to think she'd be right at the top of his payback list, with interest, when the money did arrive."

Suzanna clutched her head, digging her fingers into her thick hair. "This is so absurd I don't even know where to begin. All the sacrifices I made, all the extra hours I worked. You think my supporting Harris and Claudia was part of some greed-driven plot?"

"Let's just say I think you know a good opportunity when you see it." His hawkish eyes traveled over her, missing nothing. "You know, looking back on all that's happened these past five years, I have to say the thing that sticks in my craw most is just that—your supporting them. If you hadn't been so...so accommodating," he mocked, "they would've grown tired of the struggle and separated years ago. You made it possible for them to survive. No, you slapped an ironclad guarantee on it. I blame you, Miss Keating, for robbing my father and me of Harris's last years."

Her throat closed up tight, and when she spoke her words came out in a croak. "That's so unfair. You brought on your misery all by yourselves. Tell me, do you blame his death on me, too?" She wanted him to say no, but he didn't.

"All I have to say is there's nothing to be gained by continuing your pursuit of us."

"M-my what?"

"I'm referring to Timothy. You'll gain nothing more than what I just offered."

Suzanna's trembling grew to a visible shaking. "Get out!" She pointed to the waiting limousine. "Leave, right this instant!"

A frown worked over Logan's brow and down to his mouth. "I can see this matter isn't going to get settled here. I was wrong. I should've listened to my attorneys and let them handle it. I'm sorry, Miss Keating."

Something about the way he said "I'm sorry" raised the hair on her arms. He wasn't apologizing for wasting these past few minutes. He was looking ahead to something that still hadn't happened.

He turned and started down the steps.

"Wait. Attorneys? What are you talking about?"

He stopped on the walk, squinting up at her through the thick August sunlight, his long glossy hair lying like ruffled feathers where his fingers had combed through. For a moment Suzanna lost the thread of their argument and merely stared. Without a doubt, Logan Bradford was the most compellingly sensual man she'd ever met, and where that conclusion came from she had no idea. Considering the argument they were embroiled in, she was appalled at herself for thinking it.

"D-do you intend to pursue this issue?" she stammered.

"Timmy's guardianship? Of course. I was hoping to avoid going to court. That's why I wanted to speak with you in person. But..." He shrugged, waiting for the word "court" to take root.

But Suzanna would not be intimidated. "Well, Mr. Bradford, if that's what it takes to keep Timmy with me—" her fiery eyes met his levelly "—then I'll see you in court."

He tilted his head to one side in a sort of nod to acknowledge the invisible gauntlet lying between them on the hot cracked walk. Then he returned to his car and a moment later was gone.

Laundry still sagged from back-window lines and children continued to squabble just as before, but for Suzanna the world had suddenly spun off its axis. She slumped to the top step and braced her head in her trembling hands.

All her life she'd been the responsible daughter. The helper her father had depended on in the store after school. The friend her mother had leaned on when her father died. The mentor Claudia had turned to with her troubles.

And, of course, the house would be hers, her father had always said—whether she wanted it or not. The business, too—and all its attendant headaches. She was the good girl, the sensible girl, the one who could handle anything.

Suzanna gazed at the white summer sky, blinking back tears. Well, she had news for whoever was dumping this latest problem on her. She'd had enough, thank you. She was getting tired.

Besides, she had the sinking feeling she'd finally run into a problem she could *not* handle. And its name was Logan Bradford.

CHAPTER TWO

LOGAN BRADFORD folded his white linen napkin into a fan and waggled it across a puddle of sunshine, enjoying the play of light and shadow within its creases. From high above the breezy porch came the caw of gulls, a sound as constant and familiar as the beat of his heart. Idly he lifted his eyes and caught sight of a snowy egret riding a low wind inland over the dunes. Leaning his chair back until it rocked on two legs, he followed the flight until the bird banked into the reeds and disappeared from sight. Logan sighed, wishing he could be out there himself.

But he couldn't—his chair dropped back into place with a dull thunk—and there was no sense wishing for what couldn't be. They had a job to do today, a major problem to address, and as usual it was up to him to spearhead the campaign. He tossed aside the napkin and focused again on the discussion.

"Of course she has a case," Charlie Gibbons was saying from the opposite side of the table, "and we'd be foolish to ignore it." Charlie had served as legal counsel to the family for more than thirty years.

"A case? On what grounds?" Collin Bradford asked with imperious disdain. He crushed out his cigarette as if he wanted to ram it through the table. Logan hadn't seen his father this agitated in years.

"She's the boy's primary care-giver, Collin, that's what grounds."

"I don't give a damn who she is. We're talking about my grandson here, a Bradford." Then, in a mutter of contempt, "Even if his gene pool *is* slightly polluted. And I'll not have him raised in a slum by a culturally bankrupt, socially retarded—"

"Collin, your blood pressure," Logan warned. And when the old man still wouldn't be quiet, "Father!"

Collin spun on him. "What?" he snapped. "What?"

"Calm down. We won't get anywhere with you flying off the handle."

His father snorted, grumbled and shifted his weight, but finally settled back.

"So, what approach do you suggest we take?" Logan asked, glancing from Charlie to the two other lawyers who'd made the sixty-mile trek south from Boston for this conference—on a Saturday, no less.

Eagerly they sat forward now that they had his attention. Or thought they had it. But Logan was having difficulty concentrating this afternoon. His thoughts kept straying to Harris, who ultimately was the cause of all this trouble. Young Harry, the maverick of the family who'd given them fits from the day he was born.

Harry could've had the world on a platter if only he'd been more reasonable, if only he'd listened to them. And they'd been right, too. Twenty-one was far too young for a man to get married, especially a man who had so much to lose in a divorce.

But then, Harry had had a record of defying them, hadn't he, and they shouldn't have been surprised. There was that year he took out of high school to go hiking the Pacific coast; the bonfire on the town beach that got him arrested; the senseless string of purchases, from motorcycles to exotic parrots; and then there was that decision to study photography. Not that Logan found anything wrong with photography per se, although Collin had been arguing for economics; Logan's objection sprang simply from the feckless nature of Harry's decision. Harry had driven through life without a road map, his only plan to avoid every route Logan or Collin suggested he take.

Logan scraped back his chair and paced to the far end of the porch where his gaze could roam freely, from the endless blue ocean to the south, over acres of beach and meadow and pond, all the way to the thick green woods to the north. In the milky August sunlight, Mattashaum was spread before him with a beauty that was piercing. This had been Harry's, too, his home, his legacy, reaching back nearly three hundred years. How could he have given it all up?

"Logan?" the lawyer who'd been speaking called.

Without turning Logan nodded. "I'm listening. Go on."

But he wasn't listening very attentively. Mostly his thoughts were directed toward the past, toward the fighting and threats and eventually the effect Harry had had on their father's health. Logan wondered once again what might have happened if he'd been here to mediate when Collin and Harry had started their battle. But he'd been in California on business, investigating wind farms and a factory that would become the prototype for his own, and by the time he'd returned Collin and Harry were entrenched, their anger having reached the point of no return.

Logan had tried to talk some sense into his younger brother, tried to tell him not to be so obstinate, that he was pushing the old man too far. Collin could be handled if one was understanding and patient, and if Harry really wanted this girl, he should stop arguing and let a few years pass for Collin to get used to the idea. In the meantime he should finish college and work himself into a more independent position.

But no, Harry couldn't wait, said it was high time somebody in the family had backbone—a remark that still rankled. He'd thumbed his nose at Collin's threats of disinheritance, then went ahead and married the girl.

Logan chose not to contact Harry after Collin's heart attack. For one thing, he'd been too busy tending their father and taking over the running of Mattashaum. But mostly he'd been too angry and had feared he might say something he'd be sorry for later, something spiteful, like the heart attack had been all Harry's fault. As angry as he'd been, he hadn't wanted to do that. Guilt was a terrible weapon to wield, and Harry would come around in his own good time, he'd thought. Within a couple of months he'd grow tired of the girl, tired of his diminished life-style. He'd mature and return to the family fold.

Only problem was Suzanna Keating had stepped into the picture, doing her utmost to make the marriage work. As a consequence, months had lengthened into years, and years slipped off into forever....

Logan sighed, his broad muscled shoulders rising and falling with a sharp slump. *Ah, Harry. Why did you do it?* he implored the noisy wheel of gulls overhead. *So many harsh words, so much unnecessary pain...and you would've forgotten her soon enough. True, she was uncommonly pretty, but she was still just a schoolboy crush like so many others you'd had.*

And where did all your stubborn principles get you, little brother? Five years of living in a cramped city tenement. Five years of brain-numbing work that put your real life on hold. When you should've been studying and traveling. When you should've been waltzing with some young unencumbered beauty at a yacht-club dance. When you should have been taking on one of the family businesses or maybe...helping me.

Logan ached with a weariness that had no rational cause—except that he missed his brother so damn much and wished things hadn't ended the way they had, with the two of them still not speaking. At the time, though, he'd thought he was doing the right thing. Tough love it was called—standing back and watching someone you cared about put himself through a meat grinder in the hope he'd come out a better person on the other side. It hadn't been easy, and on more than one occasion Logan had almost caved in. But he never did. And then ... then Harry died.

Logan closed his eyes against the memory. It was best not to dwell on regrets. The past was past, and there was nothing anyone could do to change it. Besides, he had this guardianship issue to contend with right now—again thanks to Harry—and it looked like it wasn't going to be the easy uncontested move he'd originally envisioned.

Actually it was Collin who came up with the idea first. Harris's son belonged here, he said, and once Collin had said it, Logan wondered why he hadn't thought of it himself. Of course the boy should be here. With their resources, they could provide for him infinitely better than the aunt could. But more than that, it would be good for Collin to have his grandson with him. Since Harris's death, he'd aged visibly, and Logan was beginning to fear another heart attack. The boy would give him a reason to get up in the morning, get out in the fresh air and exercise, and maybe look on life with a sweeter more hopeful disposition.

Initially Collin had wanted to apply for guardianship himself, but because of his advanced age and poor health, he didn't stand a chance. Thus, Logan found himself pressed into service, which he really didn't mind; in fact, he felt rather good about it, sort of a gift he could give his aging father.

But that had been before he'd realized he'd be pitched in conflict—right opposite Suzanna Keating, that green-eyed beauty who'd upset his peace of mind from the moment he'd first laid eyes on her. If Claudia had been pretty, then her older sister was a knockout.

She had hair that spiraled from root to tip in a rich sable cloud to the middle of her back, and eyelashes so thick and sooty they cast shadows on her cheeks. Her skin was peach velvet, her bone structure chipped ice, and just to one side

of her full delicately bowed upper lip was a small beauty
mark that caused a man to stare. All the rest of her was
long, long and graceful and elegant: her neck, her arms, her
legs, her waist; even her hands were long. But good Lord,
could she fill out a T-shirt!

"Logan?" Collin's voice scraped across his reverie.
"Logan, come sit."

Logan shook himself back to the here and now and
turned. The four men at the table were staring at him. He
smiled wearily. "Where were we?"

"Strategy," Charlie Gibbons supplied. "You do agree we
should emphasize what we can provide the boy—"

"And she can't," the lawyer sitting next to him put in.

"Yes, of course." Logan took his seat. What the devil
had he been doing standing there daydreaming? Suzanna
Keating might be a beautiful young woman, but so what?
He knew lots of beautiful women and had to remember who
this one was. "I agree with everything you've said, except
that I think Tom should do the investigative work on her,
not you, Charlie. I need you to pull together an in-depth
report of our assets."

Smiles entered eyes all around the table, and the only
thing Logan had done was sit forward in a purposeful pose.

Ben, the newest member of the legal team, went so far as
to chuckle. "Man, I hope she knows what she's getting
into."

Tom added, "She should've taken you up on your offer
yesterday." Everyone shook their heads incredulously.

Everyone, that is, except Logan. He squinted out toward
the horizon, feeling uneasy. He hadn't known about Collin's offering Claudia money five years ago and had felt like
a fool repeating the ploy. Seen through Suzanna's eyes, he'd
also felt pretty crass—which should have made him angry.
He didn't enjoy being called—what did she say?—a condescending jerk? Instead of angry, however, her low opinion
of him only made him sad, a feeling that baffled him. Nor-

mally he didn't care what anyone thought. If he was angry at all, it was with Collin for having suggested the idea of paying her off in the first place.

"I still don't understand it," Ben added. "Why is she so insistent on fighting for custody when giving up the boy would be so much more to her advantage? I mean, she's single, she's unmarried. You'd think she'd be glad to be free of the responsibility."

Collin lit another cigarette, the gold lighter trembling in his thin mottled hand. "She probably thinks we'll offer a higher settlement if she stands her ground. That, or maybe she thinks if she wins the boy we'll pay her a monthly allowance for his support."

"So it's money?" Ben asked. "Is that what you're saying?"

"Of course. What else?"

Logan took the cigarette from his father and, crushing it out, added, "She might've even figured out that Harris's three million dollars is still sitting in the bank waiting to be passed on to his son."

Ben blinked and fussed with his glasses, trying to hide his surprise. "Three million! Oh, my!"

"But it'll be a cold day in hell before *she* gets hold of it," Collin blared. "That money's in *my* name, and I will not put it in Timothy's until I'm assured we've won permanent custody."

"This isn't just about money, not for us," Logan cut in, hoping to dispel the impression Collin was giving. "It's about a child being raised a certain way." He frowned thoughtfully. "But let's take money, for example, since we're already on the subject. There's always been an understanding in our family that money carries responsibility, that it should be used wisely, productively and ultimately to keep Mattashaum in one piece. We grow up learning not to squander things. We work hard, have strong values, and if my brother's son is eventually going to think like a Bradford, then he had better be raised by one, too."

He sat back, slightly embarrassed by how pompous he must sound. But more than embarrassed, he was filled with a renewed conviction that they were doing the right thing. "Charlie, let's get moving on this immediately. Can you arrange a court date within the next week?"

The lawyer reared back.

"Do whatever you have to. We should move fast, strike hard, before the opposition can muster any sort of defense."

Charlie stood up. "I'll get on the phone right now. In the meantime, Ben, run your idea by Logan. You know, the marriage angle?"

"What marriage angle?" Logan asked warily.

"Well, it isn't that we don't already have a good case," Ben said, "but we'd have an even stronger one if you were, say, engaged and planning to be married."

Logan couldn't help laughing. "Are you out of your mind?"

Collin's face crinkled into unfamiliar lines. "A marvelous idea. We could get Cecily—"

"Cecily!"

"Of course. You two've been going together since you were teenagers."

"Father, we've been friends. Nothing more."

"Logan, you're thirty-two. Isn't it time you gave some thought to having an heir or two of your own?"

"Yes, well, when I do, it won't be with Cecily Knight. Good Lord, that girl's as dumb as a bucket."

"May be, but that isn't always such a bad quality in a wife," Collin said. Everyone laughed. "Keeps them home and loyal."

Logan tried not to think about his mother who hadn't been home in twenty-four years and certainly hadn't been loyal. "I don't want a lapdog, Father."

"You could do worse. At least Cecily comes with a pedigree."

Tom smiled. "And money, I presume?"

The old man nodded. "Enough so that we know she wouldn't be after ours."

Ben chuckled and launched into some related anecdote. While he talked, Logan again found his mind drifting.

What *was* he looking for in a woman? Was he looking at all? Without any warning, an image of Suzanna Keating flashed across his mind. He flicked his head to shake away the nonsense. True, he found her physically attractive, but beyond that, they had absolutely nothing in common. And even if they did, good Lord, circumstances made a relationship with her completely untenable. So why the hell had the idea even entered his mind?

"Look, Logan, we're not saying you have to marry this Cecily," Ben said. "Just pretend to be engaged. Is she a close-enough friend to go along with the idea?"

Logan nodded, not at all sure this was such a good plan. Cecily already felt too proprietarial about him, and Collin would only encourage the match.

"Well, by all means let's get her on the phone and apprised of the situation," Ben encouraged. "Believe me, this is a trump card."

"Most definitely," Tom agreed, just as Charlie returned from making his call.

"Would you believe we have a court date next Friday?" he said. A whoop went up around the table.

Logan glanced at his father and noticed he was smiling, an occurrence that didn't happen often these days. Unexpectedly his heart swelled. He placed his hand over Collin's, squeezed it a little and smiled back. Yes, it would be good for Collin to have his grandson here. He needed something to fill the void left by Harris's death. And there wasn't a doubt in Logan's mind that the boy would be better off, too.

So, he'd go to court, all guns blazing. He'd go along with the charade that he and Cecily were engaged if that would serve the cause. He'd even ignore the tiny voice that was telling him it wasn't wise to tangle with a woman he found so attractive. Harris's son would bring new life to Mattashaum. But even more, Collin would not be let down again. At least he had one son he could depend on.

"SUZANNA KEATING?" The lawyer leaned over his desk, hand outstretched. He was a stranger to her, someone chosen at random from the phone book. She'd never had to deal with lawyers before.

"Thank you for seeing me on such short notice, Mr. Quinn." Suzanna shook his hand. He was middle-aged, with thick dark hair and a kind open face.

"My pleasure. And please call me Ray. Have a seat." He returned to his own leather chair and, picking up a memo pad, skimmed the note written there. "Hmm. A custody case," he murmured. "But not a divorce." He looked up. "How about if we start at the beginning. Whose child are we dealing with?"

She pulled in a shaky breath. "My sister's. His name is Timothy Bradford, and he's four years old. Claudia—that was my sister—and her husband were killed last May in an automobile accident."

"Oh." The lawyer's smiling face sobered. "I'm sorry to hear that. My condolences to you."

Suzanna felt a tide of emotion rising inside her. But this was neither the time nor place to cave in. She was here to do a job and needed to be strong and objective.

"I was baby-sitting Timmy when I got the news. I babysat for them all the time. Claudia and Harris used to live in the apartment right upstairs from me. That night I moved Timmy's things downstairs and he's been with me ever since. Until recently I thought he always would be."

"Did your sister leave a will naming you his guardian?"

Frowning, she shook her head.

"And you haven't done anything to have yourself...?"

"No. But I intended to someday. I just didn't realize the matter was so urgent."

"Are you his closest blood relative?"

"Yes, though he also has an uncle and a grandfather. On his father's side." She opened her purse and drew out the papers she'd received in the mail from the Bradfords the previous day, but didn't hand them over quite yet. "The uncle is now trying to become Timmy's legal guardian, and...and I guess that's why I'm here."

"Hmm." The lawyer tilted his head. "Hard feelings between the families?"

Suzanna rolled her eyes expressively.

"Tell me about it." Quinn linked his hands atop his head and sat back, his leather chair creaking.

Suzanna swallowed over a dry lump in her throat. "Well, Harris was from a well-to-do family. Their name's Bradford, and they live out on Mattashaum Harbor. Last century, one of their ancestors owned a mill here in the city. You might know the name from that."

"Oh, yes, of course."

"My sister met Harris during her freshman year at Brown University. Claudia was very bright and won lots of scholarships. That's how we could afford Brown. She lived with me and commuted, which also helped."

"I see. Uh...she lived with you?"

"Yes. My parents are deceased."

"Hmm. Seems you've assumed a lot of responsibility for someone your age." He paused. "Which is?"

"Twenty-seven."

"And single, I presume?"

She nodded hesitantly. "That won't matter, will it? My being single?"

"You'd have a stronger case if you were married, but no, I don't foresee it being a problem. So, continue. Your sister and Harris met in college. . . ."

"Yes. And fell in love at first sight, which would've been fine except they got the notion that they wanted to be married, too, right away. I tried to talk them out of it. I mean, Harris still had his senior year ahead of him, and Claudia was only eighteen. And if I may be honest, I really thought they were an unlikely match, coming from such dissimilar backgrounds. But Harris assured me that love would conquer all." Her lips twisted in a wry smile. "He also claimed that being married wouldn't create any financial hardship, but of course at the time he was assuming he'd have his family's continued support. What he didn't realize was that his father would have an entirely different view of the matter." She couldn't restrain the bitterness that slid into her tone.

"Collin Bradford saw red when Harris took my sister home to meet him. Apparently Claudia didn't pass muster. Not socially or financially acceptable I think were his words. Right there in her presence he said that, and then he accused her of being a gold digger. He vowed the marriage would never take place, and then before he could even get to know her, he threw them both out the door."

"Nice guy," the lawyer said wryly.

"A peach. Later he tried to buy Claudia off. Offered her twenty thousand dollars if she promised to stop seeing Harris." Suzanna paused while an image flashed through her mind: Logan Bradford standing on her porch offering her the same bribe. She wanted to feel resentful, but mostly she was just disappointed. Her reaction dismayed her. Why should it matter to her that he wasn't a more honorable man?

Ray Quinn cleared his throat. "Obviously your sister didn't take the money."

"No, of course not. So the old man changed direction and threatened to cut off Harris's allowance. When Harris still refused to comply, Collin said he'd dissolve all Harris's rights to his trust fund. Not only that, he'd no longer consider him part of the family." Suzanna lowered her gaze and smoothed the folds of her skirt. "I'll always admire Harris for his courage. He was only twenty-one at the time. That had to be a terrifying prospect."

"And quite a compliment to your sister."

Suzanna lifted her eyes and smiled wanly. "It *was* kind of nice, wasn't it? Being willing to give up everything just to be with the woman he loved."

"Mmm. You don't come across ardor like that too often these days."

Suzanna swallowed. "Funny you should call it ardor. Most people would call it stupidity. Harris lost everything. His father wasn't bluffing."

The lawyer grimaced. "What did they do?"

"Well, after they were married, I offered them the apartment on the second floor of my house."

"Oh, you own the house?"

She nodded, smiling. "My parents left it to me. They used to say, 'Own a three-decker and you'll always have security.'"

"That's good. That you own your own place. Very good. Go on. They came to live with you...."

"Yes, they had nowhere else to turn. Harris got a job waiting tables, bless him, and somehow finished college." The "somehow" had been with Suzanna's help, charging them no rent, cosigning his loans, even paying their utility bills.

"Did Claudia continue her education, too?"

"Not right away. What she did do right away was get pregnant."

"That couldn't have helped matters any."

"Without medical insurance? You got that right." She paused, swallowed and quietly admitted, "It was rough."

"And I'm beginning to think I know who it was roughest on," Quinn said pointedly.

"I didn't mind. Really I didn't. In fact, I loved being such an integral part of their lives. And the baby—" warmth flooded through her "—he was pure joy. Claudia returned to classes part-time, and I took care of him while she was gone."

"That, too?"

"I work out of my house, a catering business, so it was no trouble."

Ray Quinn rested his chin on his hand and smiled at her. "Are you for real?"

"Pardon me?"

"What are you doing for dinner tonight? For that matter, what are you doing for the rest of your life?"

Suzanna felt her cheeks warm as she stared at the wedding band on his left hand.

He laughed. "No, no, not me. I'm quite happily married. But I do have a fifteen-year-old son I'd love you to meet. Tell me, what are your thoughts on waiting a few years for a younger man?"

Suzanna blushed even harder.

"Sorry, I didn't mean to embarrass you." He smiled, paused, then turned his thoughts back to business.

"So, it's apparent that, aside from his parents, you've been the child's closest contact."

"Yes, since birth. And I mean that literally. I was in the delivery room when he was born."

"That right?"

She nodded, beaming. "It was wonderful."

The lawyer picked up a pencil and pensively tapped its eraser end on the desk. "Tell me about the uncle. So far you haven't mentioned him except to say he's the one who's suing for guardianship. What's his story?"

Suzanna blinked against another flurry of unbidden images: Logan unbuttoning his jacket and brushing it aside; Logan sweeping her up in his heavy-lidded stare; Logan's strong hands, his full lower lip, the sun glinting through his hair....

She sucked in her breath. Heavenly day, how could this be happening? How could she dislike someone so completely and yet experience this traitorous flight of fancy?

Discomfited by the heat rising in her cheeks, she coughed and cleared her throat. "Um, well, he lives with his father out at Mattashaum...."

"Just the two of them?"

"Yes. And staff. His mother left years ago, when the boys were little. She was younger than her husband and considerably more ... human. Harris used to say it was his father's coldness that drove her away. I think she's remarried and living in Texas. In any case, she's out of the picture."

"I see. So, what role did the uncle play in your sister's travails?"

"The same role the father played. They're joined at the hip—in business, in attitudes, in everything. To be honest, Logan wasn't at Mattashaum when Claudia visited, so he wasn't part of the original argument, but she did meet him later. He visited Harris at Brown a few times to persuade him not to get married, and it was quite obvious he'd sided with their father unquestioningly. At first Harris couldn't get over it. He'd thought he and Logan were closer than that, but somehow, somewhere, his brother had changed. Harris claimed it was because Logan is next in line to inherit Mattashaum, and he didn't want to do anything to fall out of their father's good graces. Whatever the reason, after the marriage, he never talked to Harris again. That hurt Harris a lot."

The lawyer listened with an increasingly censorious expression working into his features. "Sounds like they're into playing control games in a major way."

"Exactly!" Suzanna came alive. "That's what Harris always said. His father needed control over the people around him, especially his family. That was his real objection to Claudia—she'd gained a control over Harris that he didn't have. And so he did what he did—tossed Harris out without a dime, knowing he had college to finish, nowhere to live, a wife and child to support—all with the cold-blooded purpose simply of breaking him." Suzanna lowered her eyes. "I don't want Timmy growing up in that sort of environment."

Ray Quinn heaved a long sigh. "This Logan—you say he hasn't had any contact with the boy?"

"Uh-uh. He's a total stranger to Timmy."

The lawyer sat back in his chair, stretching comfortably. "Suzanna, this is going to be a piece of cake. What are you so worried about?"

She bit her lip, then handed over the document she'd received the previous day.

Quinn opened the envelope, skimmed the letter, then tossed it onto his desk. "All right, so they're taking the issue to court. Don't get upset. Not yet, anyway." But seeing she was already upset, he sat forward, arms folded on the desk.

"Okay, this is what's going to happen. Next Friday you and I are going to meet with this Logan Bradford and his attorney in a judge's chamber, and the purpose of that meeting is for the judge to name one of you temporary guardian—someone has to have immediate legal custody of the child. And what that judge is going to do is rule in your favor because you're the person closest to Timmy, the one who's been giving him care all along."

"Are you sure?"

"I've never heard of a case where it didn't work out that way. It's what's best for the child. And I'll bet you're going to win the permanent-custody hearing on the same grounds, too."

"Permanent-custody hearing? When will that be?"

He shrugged. "Could be as long as a year from now, but probably sooner. In the meantime you and Bradford will be investigated—"

"By whom?" she interrupted, sitting up straighter.

"Oh, a social worker, maybe a psychologist. Someone appointed by the court. It's routine."

"And what exactly will this person be investigating?"

"Your home, your habits, your attitudes toward raising a child. Lots of things. Don't worry, I'll help you prepare for it. Then at the final hearing, the investigator's report will be used as evidence—partial evidence," he amended, "of your suitability as a guardian."

She gulped. "And where'll the rest of the evidence come from?"

"Me. But we'll cross that bridge when we come to it. Right now stop worrying. Timmy's not going anywhere as a result of next Friday's hearing."

"He'd better not. After everything he's been through, I can't imagine the harm it would do."

"And that's exactly what we're going to emphasize to the judge. Is there anything else? You still look worried."

"Your fee. How much is this going to cost me? I know going to court doesn't come cheap."

He told her and she gulped. Though the fee was reasonable, it was more than she could handle.

"We'll work out payments. How's that?"

She nodded, wishing she could will this entire distressful predicament to disappear. "Am I done here?"

"Almost." From a desk drawer he pulled out a sheaf of printed forms and a small tape recorder. "Except that now we're going to go through your story again, from the beginning, in even greater detail...."

CHAPTER THREE

SUZANNA DRESSED carefully for the hearing in a conservative navy dress with a long paisley jacket and matching navy pumps and handbag. She brushed back her long hair and secured it neatly at her nape with a wide gold clasp. Simple gold earrings and a light touch of makeup finished off what she hoped was a look that would convince the judge she was suitable guardian material.

"You look great," Ray Quinn said when she met him at his office. "We're gonna knock 'em dead."

Now, sitting beside him at the long thickly varnished table in the judge's chamber, she wasn't so sure. They were waiting for the Bradford party to arrive, and with each passing minute, her stomach knotted tighter—which was probably the very effect they hoped to achieve with their dramatic tardiness.

When they finally did show up, Suzanna wished they'd stayed away indefinitely. Where she had tiptoed in, peeking around the door first and feeling decidedly nauseated, they marched in like a flank of an attacking army. So many of them too, headed up, of course, by Logan Bradford.

Suzanna's eyes swept from his long neatly combed brown hair down over his authoritative pin-striped suit and aggressively red tie, and back up to his stern sun-bronzed face. As if he sensed he was being watched, he looked in her direction, and a jolt of electricity shot through her. The knot in her stomach quivered, along with her hands and her shoulder muscles and just about every other part of her, too.

Quickly she glanced away, assuring herself her reaction was merely nerves and adrenaline.

In Logan's wake marched three austere-looking men carrying briefcases. They were followed by an exceptionally pretty blonde dressed in a blue Chanel suit. Suzanna frowned, wondering who she was and why she looked so familiar. Finally came an elderly gentleman who could be none other than Collin Bradford.

Collin was a tall man, nearly six feet, who walked ramrod straight even with the assistance of a cane. He was thin, almost gaunt, and pale, but there was no denying he'd been a handsome man in his youth. His suit was meticulous, and his white hair groomed so fastidiously that his pink scalp showed through where his comb had left furrows. His mouth was hard, his bearing imperious, and in a flash of insight Suzanna realized that this group was not so much being led into the room by Logan Bradford as it was being herded forward by the cane-wielding man at its rear.

Without hesitation the Bradford party scraped back chairs and claimed the opposite side of the table: Logan near the judge, who sat at the table's head, then the pretty blonde, and next to her the three lawyers. That filled their side, leaving the end chair, the one that faced the judge, for Collin Bradford. When he sat, he and the judge exchanged loaded glances. Suzanna wondered if the judge was perturbed by Collin's choice of seat, seeing it perhaps as a statement. While it might be interpreted as a power play, Suzanna didn't figure that Collin had much choice. She doubted he'd sit on her side any more readily than she'd sit on his.

Briefcases snapped open, steel-rimmed glasses were hooked into place—and Suzanna's heart sank. Never had she felt so out of her league.

A reassuring hand settled on her shoulder. She looked at her attorney and tried to return his smile, but her feelings of foreboding continued to grow. Harris had always said his family was overwhelming when they set their minds to something and that the only way to survive was to get out of their way. She was beginning to understand what he'd meant.

The judge bid them a perfunctory good-morning and started the proceedings.

Ray Quinn presented her case admirably, she thought, delivering all the salient information she'd given him. He emphasized the fact that she owned her own home, that she ran her own business, and that the nature of that business allowed her to be with Timmy almost all the time, and when she did have to leave him behind to cater an event, a baby-sitter was readily available on the third floor.

But what she found especially impressive was the impassioned manner in which he argued the importance of Timmy's staying with her, the bearing that continuous care had on his psychological health and the harm that would come from uprooting him and placing him with strangers. When Ray finished, Suzanna sagged with relief. No one, she was sure, could've done a better job.

But then the judge turned his attention to the Bradford side of the table, and before they were even a minute into their presentation, she was sitting on the edge of her chair, filled with dread once again.

They were sharks, cunning and vicious, even while presenting a most dignified, businesslike front. With the cold precision of statistics, they ripped apart Suzanna's life-style, citing the ever increasing crime rate in her neighborhood, the impoverished local school system, even the poor quality of the air and water the child would be subjected to if he remained in her care. They had photographs of her house, which granted, needed a paint job, but which they claimed was dangerously substandard. They produced financial records that argued she wasn't as solvent as she seemed, that, rather, she had needed to take an equity loan the previous year. They disclosed the fact that the baby-sitter on the third floor was a seventeen-year-old dropout with a record of drug abuse. And finally they finished off with the opinion that, working as many hours as she did, Suzanna couldn't possibly give Timmy the attention and quality care he needed and deserved.

Suzanna felt so heated with frustration by the time they were done she wondered why she didn't just go up in flames. What she did do was train her furious gaze on Logan Bradford and somehow find the courage to say, "This isn't right."

Everyone's attention turned to her, but she paid them no heed. Her argument was with the man who had hired these lawyers and poured his venom into them. "It isn't fair. Nothing you've said is true. It's all half-truths or outright lies coated over with statistics or sleek legalese. My house, for instance. Almost everything's up to code in my house—wiring, fire-alarm system, security locks. The only thing I haven't overhauled yet is the plumbing, but nobody's life is in danger because of that.

"As far as Timmy's education goes, I plan to send him to the parish school. Not that that should matter at this particular hearing. At the next, sure..."

Across the table, Logan Bradford's left eyebrow arched in the incredulous curve that seemed to be his hallmark. His haughty attitude only stoked her anger.

"Furthermore, that so-called dropout who *occasionally* baby-sits Timmy is attending night school for her GED and she never abused drugs. Once, *once,* she was caught with a marijuana cigarette and got called into the principal's office, but she hasn't touched the stuff since."

"Suzanna," her lawyer admonished softly, patting her arm. He'd advised her to let him do all the talking, but she couldn't just sit here and do nothing. They'd slandered her!

"And one more thing," she said, shaking Quinn off. "I took that loan in order to help Harris set up his own photography studio. It wasn't because I couldn't afford to pay my bills. It was something extra."

She noticed Logan blink and for one brief moment thought an emotion flickered through his normally unreadable expression. Something in the eyes. Surprise? Guilt? But then he returned with, "And we both know why you went to such measures to help my brother, don't we?" and she knew she'd seen nothing.

"Mr. Bradford, Ms. Keating," the judge exhorted. "This isn't a forum to vent personal differences. Now, could we return to the matter at hand?"

Suzanna's lawyer apologized for her outburst but agreed with her opinion that the opposition had taken an unfair tack. Much to Suzanna's surprise, the judge concurred and reminded the Bradford team that they were there to state why Logan Bradford would make a good guardian, not to prove that the opposition would make a bad one.

But the warning had come too late; the words had already been spoken. With a smugness that made Suzanna want to scream, Logan's lawyers continued, doing exactly what the judge had bid. Now, after the damage was done, they presented the sort of life the child could expect if he went to live with Logan Bradford: a twenty-room house on a private three-hundred-acre estate by the ocean; a personal nanny whose only duty would be to cater to his needs; a housekeeper, caretakers, horses and boats; an education at an exclusive country day school. And then they pulled out their big ammunition: lifelong financial security in the form of a three-million-dollar trust fund; the love of a retired grandfather; and most importantly, Logan Bradford himself. Logan, they said, would provide Timmy with the male influence that he currently lacked and that a boy obviously needed. Moreover, since Logan was engaged to marry Cecily Knight, the woman sitting next to him, he'd soon be able to provide the stability and nurturing warmth of family life, as well.

Suzanna's gaze shot up. Logan Bradford was engaged? For some perverse reason, her heart sank.

His eyes flicked to hers, flicked away, flicked back. Despite the defiant angle of his jaw, she noticed the tips of his ears turn pink. Curious, she took a closer look at the young woman whose arm was now loyally looped through his. Of course. She was the same girl who'd attended that party two and a half years ago as his date.

Disappointment pressed on Suzanna's heart, a feeling she attributed to the clout this new bit of information added to Logan's case. With an effort she turned her attention back to the concluding words being delivered by the oldest of the Bradford lawyers.

In a compassionate almost apologetic tone, he was conceding the possibility that initially the move might upset the boy. "But in the long run the benefits will far outweigh the temporary upset. Timothy is young and will soon adjust."

At the head of the table, the judge removed his glasses and pressed his fingertips against his eye sockets. He looked tired. "First, let me remind you that the decision I'm about to hand over is only temporary. I also want to say that decisions of this sort are always difficult for me, and painful. But in this case, especially so. My heart grieves for the child, so recently orphaned, and I want to state clearly that my decision is being made solely with his best interests in mind." He folded his hands on the table and took a deep breath.

Suzanna closed her eyes, praying with all her might.

"Ms. Keating, you've obviously played an important role in little Timothy's life, and the care you've given him has been both loving and generous."

Her heart began to lift.

"But I'd be remiss if I ignored the fact that you do work long hours, do live in an increasingly undesirable neighborhood, and your finances are somewhat strained.

"For those reasons, and because of the quality care and stable environment Mr. Bradford is clearly able to provide,

I feel compelled to deny your appeal for temporary guardianship and to grant it, instead, to him.''

Suzanna gasped, pressing a hand to the pain slashing through her chest. For several long seconds she couldn't catch her breath.

Opposite her, the Bradford contingent took the news with no surprise, no expressions of relief or joy. Winning was what they were used to. The surprise would have been if they'd lost.

She noticed Logan watching her, gloating, no doubt. She lowered her head, shading her eyes with an unsteady hand.

"However," the judge intoned, "considering the close emotional bond between Ms. Keating and the child, I'm granting her liberal visitation rights."

Suzanna was still trying to make sense of what she'd just heard when, from the end of the table, a deep voice boomed, "No!" She jumped and turned, as did everyone else, to find Collin Bradford on his feet.

"I'll not allow it, Drum—"

"What do you mean, you won't allow it?" The judge's eyes widened with a silent caution. "Sit down, Mr. Bradford." His stare was quelling.

He then turned to Logan. "You've heard Mr. Quinn's testimony regarding the importance of continuous care to the emotional well-being of a child. I urge you to put aside whatever rancor may exist between the two families and enter a time of cooperation. We're talking about a child here, a little human being who's emotionally quite fragile right now. Do you understand?"

Reluctantly Logan gave a short nod.

"So—" the judge braced his palms on the table "—to be specific, I want Ms. Keating to accompany the child to his new home, to stay with him until she's sufficiently satisfied that he's comfortable with his surroundings and to visit him often, every day if possible, all day if necessary."

From the corner of her eye, she saw Collin Bradford's thin aristocratic face darken with anger. But her attention, for the most part, was concentrated on Logan. He remained unmoved, or almost so, but she did detect a tightening of his mouth and an increase in his breathing that led her to believe he was no more enamored of the judge's decision than his father was.

"Your Honor." Her voice cracked. "When does Timmy have to make this move?"

He returned a look that was sympathetic yet hooded, she thought. "As soon as possible."

"I'll pick him up the day after tomorrow," Logan said.

Suzanna wanted to protest that Sunday was too soon, but the judge was already nodding approval and saying they would be notified as soon as their final hearing was slated. Then he wished them all well and left the room.

They rose, Suzanna unsteadily. Ray clutched her arm.

"I don't understand how that happened," he said. "I really don't understand. I'm sorry, Suzanna." He seemed truly stunned.

She shook her head. "It wasn't your fault." It wasn't anybody's fault. Logan Bradford simply had the money to hire the best assassins. If anything, money had won the day. Unfortunately the one who was going to be hurt most hadn't even had a voice in the debacle.

Her stomach bottomed out. Timmy. How would she ever explain this to him?

She picked up her purse and stumbled from the table. Behind her the Bradford party was shuffling papers and snapping briefcases.

"Ray, what am I going to do?" she cried in a hoarse whisper. "I can't imagine living without Timmy. He's so much a part of me."

Her lawyer paused to place an arm around her shoulders. "Shh, shh. You'll be fine."

"And what about Timmy? The question isn't *if* he'll be frightened in his new surroundings, but *how* frightened he'll be."

Ray Quinn tightened his embrace. "This arrangement's only temporary, remember that. And I promise you, we're going to win the permanent order."

But his words were cold comfort. By the time the final hearing rolled around, the damage would already be done. Timmy would have emotional scars that might haunt him well into adulthood. Unless...

"Don't even think it," her lawyer said, holding her at arm's length and staring at her levelly.

"Think what?" She tried to feign innocence.

"About going off somewhere with Timmy where they won't be able to find you. That's kidnapping, Suzanna." His voice was quiet and deadly serious. "And kidnapping's a federal crime."

Suzanna lowered her head and two plump tears dropped to the floor. "But what am I going to do?"

"The best thing you can do now is follow the judge's advice. Cooperate and make the move as smooth as possible for Timmy. If you're upset, he'll be upset. But if you're enthusiastic, so will he be."

"But I can't. I hate it. I hate everything about it."

"For his sake, Suzanna."

"But I'll just be helping him adjust to the enemy camp. I'll be working against myself. If he adjusts and begins to like living there, I'll never get him back."

The lawyer chewed on his lip. "It is rather a catch-22, isn't it? I'm sorry, Suzanna. I don't know what else we can do."

With a hand on her back, he urged her toward the exit. But just before stepping through, she turned. Logan Bradford and his contingent were marching toward the same door, looking as if they might mow her down. His hard gray eyes met hers and held.

This isn't right! she longed to cry out. *You don't understand the harm you're doing!*

But he strode right past her, locked within his certainty that justice had been served, and the words withered on her lips.

LOGAN HIT THE PATH RUNNING.

As soon as he'd returned from the courthouse, he'd shed his suit and wing tips for a T-shirt, shorts and comfortable sneakers. Now the gravel crunched beneath his pounding feet with satisfying regularity. Wind whistled in his ears.

"Where the hell're you going, son?" Collin had demanded. "You've got Cecily here."

"No, *you've* got Cecily. You invited her. You entertain her. And while you're at it, why don't you call your old golfing buddy, Drummond Slade, and invite him over, too." He didn't often snap like that, especially at his father, which was a sure sign his nerves were really frayed.

That would pass. It would. All he needed was a good run along the beach. He didn't want to think for a while. Just pump along. One, two, one, two. No wondering how Drummond Slade had just happened to be their judge today. Just run. No thinking. One, two...

He reached the end of the gravel path and struck out over the soft sand, the long lean muscles of his legs straining with the sudden resistance. By the time he'd crossed the dunes, he was winded. He doubled over from the waist, hands braced on his thighs, trying to catch his breath.

This had never happened before, not this soon into a run, and he could only attribute it to the stress of the custody hearing. That had to be the reason he felt so drained.

Slowly he straightened and resumed his journey toward the shoreline at a contemplative walk. It had been one hell of a morning, and that had only been the warm-up. He certainly wasn't looking forward to the main event, which his lawyers assured him was going to be a no-holds-barred affair.

"Damn!" he swore, kicking a clump of brittle seaweed. He didn't like being a part of this, didn't like it at all. It was far messier than he'd expected. He'd hoped to just walk through his part, win the decision and then come home, mission accomplished. What he hadn't counted on was the effect Suzanna Keating would have on him.

"Damn!" he swore again, recalling the look she'd given him as they'd left the courthouse. She had no right to look at him like that and make him feel this way.

She hadn't known a thing about Harris's three million dollars, he was almost sure of it. Her surprise, when it was mentioned, had been too genuine. What was worse, Logan was getting the sinking feeling she didn't care about it, either, no matter how adamantly Collin insisted she did.

And the measures she'd taken to help Harris— Logan hadn't been aware of half the things she'd done. Hell, he hadn't been aware that Harris had even needed so much help. A knot of guilt tightened in his chest when he thought about how hard it must have been on her, and she couldn't have been much older than Harris himself.

She might have been acting out of self-interest, figuring that someday Collin would relent and loosen the strings on Harris's money. But Logan didn't think so. Not anymore. He grimaced as he recalled how brashly he'd stood on her porch and accused her of doing just that.

No, what they were dealing with was one of those rare individuals who acted simply out of the goodness of her heart. Generosity, that was what the virtue was called, a trait Collin just didn't comprehend. That was why he still insisted she was after something.

Only the boy. Only the boy. Logan would bet his life on it.

He stopped a moment to wipe his brow with the bottom of his shirt. Damn, he didn't like the turn his mind was taking. Suzanna Keating was an adversary, both legal and personal, and it would be dangerous for him to forget that fact. Besides, how could he be so sure she was as guileless as she appeared? She might just be a good actress. He really ought to keep his guard up. Another thing he ought to do was stop snapping at Collin and acting as if there was dissention in the ranks.

Logan resumed walking.

Still, it was a pity she'd been so defenseless. Her lawyer was local and quite mediocre, while he and Collin had had the best of Boston's best. It had been almost painful to watch.

He reached the shoreline and stood squinting out over the endless sun-shot waves. Unwittingly a smile crept into his eyes.

She'd never backed down, though. Never once was she intimidated. He could still see the flash of fury in her big green eyes, still hear her vibrant voice as she'd defended herself. Despite everything, he admired that in her. She didn't deserve the beating she took. No one did.

A wave washed in, cold water seeping through his sneakers and then through his socks. He didn't care. Suddenly he felt unclean, smeared with villainy. He walked into the thrashing water, heedless of his clothing, heedless of his watch, knowing only that he needed to swim. He'd feel better after that.

They'd won round one, and on a rational level he knew the decision was right. The boy would be far better off at Mattashaum than in the city. He wouldn't change his mind about that. Besides, he couldn't change his mind, not at this point. "Decide that you're right, and then forge ahead," Collin had always exhorted, advice that had served Logan well on more than one occasion. Moreover, Logan didn't want to change his mind. Not only would the boy be better off, but he'd also be good for Collin.

He removed his sneakers and flung them back onto the beach. Then he dived into a high curling wave, came up spluttering on the other side and kicked over onto his back. Sure, a swim. Rationally he knew he was the right person to win today's contest. After a swim he was certain to *feel* the rightness of the victory. Then he'd be able to take on whatever needed to be tackled next.

Yet, as he backstroked into deeper water, an image of Suzanna's grief-stricken face flashed across the sky, and Logan began to wonder if all the waves in all the world could ever make him feel absolved.

CHAPTER FOUR

SUZANNA WAS PUTTING away the lunch dishes when she heard footsteps on the walk. She tensed and checked her watch. Logan had phoned the previous day and said he'd be here around two. It was precisely two.

She smoothed back the tendrils of hair that had come loose from her French braid, although she knew no amount of primping would repair the damage done by two sleepless nights and two tense days of trying to keep up a cheerful front.

The doorbell buzzed, and without warning Suzanna's eyes burned with anger and grief. This was so wrong, so utterly stupidly wrong. How could the judge have made such a decision?

But of course, all he'd had to go on was the testimony presented him, and the Bradford lawyers had made quite a case. For a moment even she had almost believed that the things Logan and his father could provide with their money were more important than what she could provide with her love.

The buzzer sounded again. "Okay, I'm coming," she muttered, hurrying toward the door. She dreaded what was about to unfold. But it wouldn't last forever. She'd resigned herself to go along with the judge's wishes and cooperate; she'd certainly be pleasant in Timmy's presence to help ease his wariness, but she would never forget her purpose. If it was the last thing she ever did, she was going to win Timmy back.

Suzanna opened the entry door and forced herself to look Logan Bradford in the eye. She swallowed, struck as she always was by his overpowering good looks. Instead of the nononsense business suit he'd worn in court, today he was dressed in a blue cotton shirt, worn jeans and a pair of running shoes. His clothing went a long way toward softening the aura of power and danger she usually felt radiating off him.

She hated herself for staring, hated even more the incriminating blush warming her cheeks. Logan Bradford might be an attractive man, but he was also the man she least wanted to be attracted to.

"Come in," she said, flicking her head in a gesture of indifference.

He nodded crisply before stepping into her kitchen. "Is Timothy ready?" he asked.

"No, not quite. He's taking a nap."

His mouth tightened. "I told you I'd be here at two."

"And might I remind you that you haven't come to pick up a parcel." She paused, realizing this wasn't how she wanted the day to go. For Timmy's sake, she wanted peace.

"Have a seat, Mr. Bradford. We really ought to talk, and now that we have this moment to ourselves...."

One of Logan's dark eyebrows lifted and his wary gaze swept over her.

"Please," she added, pulling out a chair for him and taking one herself.

Still eyeing her cautiously, he sat.

She pressed her damp palms to her thighs and stared at the tabletop, wondering where to begin, knowing only she *had* to begin. Somebody had to.

"I—I'm afraid Timmy has already begun to react negatively to the move to your place. I—"

"What the devil did you tell him?"

"Lower your voice. I'm trying to converse with you, not argue. Seems to me we've done enough of that."

He scowled, then much to her surprise, nodded. "I agree. So, what's all this about negative reactions?"

"Timmy hasn't slept well the past two nights. Believe me, I broke the news to him as enthusiastically as I could. The last thing I want is for him to be upset. I described his living with you as a vacation at the beach. I pretended that I knew you and... and liked you." She looked aside, unable to hold Logan's penetrating gaze as she said this. "I even assured him he was going to have lots of fun with you.

"Still, he's confused and distressed. How could he not be? He's only a baby. Nothing overt or dramatic, mind you. He's a brave little guy and he keeps a lot to himself. He just hasn't been sleeping well. That's why he's napping now. He was tired."

Logan was quiet a moment, his hawkish gaze traveling over her. "Looks like he isn't the only one who hasn't been sleeping."

She shrugged. "Comes with the territory. You'll learn that soon enough."

He looked vaguely stunned. "I must say this new attitude of yours is a pleasant surprise."

"Yes, well, don't make the mistake of interpreting it as capitulation. I may be resigned to my nephew's leaving today—I'm not about to defy a court order—but I'll never stop fighting to get him back. Never."

They stared long and hard at each other, then almost imperceptibly Logan's eyes softened. "You can't win, you know." It wasn't a threat, more a commiseration.

She swallowed, taken off guard by this moment of honesty. "Then I'll die trying."

He gazed at her for several candid moments—looking ahead to the upcoming battle perhaps? "I wish you felt differently."

"How can I? This move is so wrong." Suzanna was struck by the absence of anger in her voice. Was she simply too drained to muster an emotional response?

She looked into his crystalline eyes and her heart pounded. "Logan?" She'd never called him by his first name before, yet she so needed to connect with him. He blinked, his eyes widening. "There are going to be repercussions. Timmy's troubled sleep is only the beginning. I thought I ought to warn you."

He leaned back, studying her cautiously. "You really don't think much of me, do you?"

"On the contrary, I think a great deal about you, most of it bad."

"I resent that." However, like Suzanna, he seemed unable to muster any deep emotional conviction. "But in the spirit of cooperation, I'll forgo arguing and merely ask why. Be honest now."

Suzanna's back straightened. "You've got to be kidding. The reasons are legion."

"Pick one, any one."

"Okay. How about the way you treated my sister."

"What about it? How *did* I treat your sister?" His eyes narrowed.

"Oh, come on. Calling her socially and financially unfit? Trying to bribe her as if all she cared about was money? Disinheriting Harris because of her?"

"*I* did all that?"

"Yes, and it was the lowest, most insulting behavior I've ever heard of."

"*I* did that," he repeated.

"Well—" she fidgeted "—your father did, but you went right along with him, which makes you just as culpable. You opposed Harris's marriage because Claudia's roots were blue collar, and where I come from that's called class bigotry."

He laughed without humor. "Now wait just a minute. I never called anyone unfit, unless it was Harris, and that was only because he was too damned young and immature to get married, so don't start calling me a class bigot, Miss Keating.''

He was starting to steam, Suzanna knew it. Yet she didn't have time to be concerned. She was too preoccupied by what he'd just said. "You opposed the marriage because of their age?''

"Of course!''

Suzanna passed an unsteady hand over her brow. Age had been her major objection, too.

Suddenly there was so much she wanted to ask Logan, so many questions blurring her convictions....

But at that moment a pair of large teary eyes peeked out at them from around the archway connecting the kitchen to the dining room. Logan's head tilted inquisitively, his gaze darting from Timmy to Suzanna.

"Timmy, come out here, love. Come on, don't be afraid. I want you to meet—'' she paused ''—your uncle Logan.''

Reluctantly the child scuffed into the kitchen, all the while glowering at Logan. Suzanna knotted with tension, wondering how Logan would handle the situation.

He'd been raised in a cold affectionless household. From such an environment, children sometimes grew into loving adults, as Harris had, their gentleness and understanding a deliberate effort to avoid repeating the past. But more often than not, children of a cold affectionless environment turned into cold affectionless adults, and Suzanna had a strong suspicion she knew which path Logan had taken.

From the corner of her eye she noticed him swallow. He got down on his haunches as the boy drew nearer.

"Hello, Tim,'' he said, looking terribly uneasy.

Timmy stopped a foot in front of him and stuck his thumb in his mouth, sucking so hard his cheeks hollowed. Neither of them said a word or made a move. Suzanna waited. And more time passed. Finally she was tempted to say, "Do something, one of you!''

But then she realized that something was indeed going on. An exploration with the eyes. A journey of the heart.

Timmy bore a strong resemblance to his father. Already Suzanna could see the same cleft in his chin, tiny though it was, the same soft gray in his eyes. Logan had to be noticing the similarities, too.

But Logan, himself, looked like Harris. Granted, his features were stronger, darker, more adult and serious, but they were similar enough to Harris's to cause the child to stare in wonder. It seemed a magic glass had slid between them and to look to the other side they each had to pass through a third image.

Ever so cautiously Timmy lifted his dimpled hand and touched it to Logan's high-boned cheek. He brushed one of Logan's dark eyebrows, brushed a shock of dark hair—and his cherry-red mouth turned down at the corners in an expression too full of sadness for any four-year-old to know.

Suzanna's throat tightened and her eyes grew hot. She wanted to scoop him up and hug him to her until all the pain was gone. Yet she didn't move, some sixth sense telling her it wasn't her place to interfere.

What she did do was pray, pray with all her heart for Logan not to hurt Timmy. The boy was obviously undergoing something profound and complex as his gaze traveled over Logan's face, as his fingertips traced the mystery in this stranger's familiar features.

Suzanna wasn't able to pinpoint the exact moment when Logan realized what Timmy was doing. He was such a master at concealing whatever he was thinking. But she did notice a muscle pull taut along his jaw, did see a frown crease his brow—and something indefinable enter his eyes. He raised a large sun-darkened hand and, as if he were reaching through that magic glass, gently placed it on Timmy's head. "Hello, Tim," he tried again.

Timmy looked up toward Suzanna, his lower lip tremulous. On some vague emotional level he must have decided that the physical similarities this man bore to his father weren't enough, perhaps were even a trick, and that Logan was really just a stranger, after all.

Logan glanced at her, too, obviously having run out of things to say. He looked so uncertain of himself she almost felt sorry for him and was confused by her urge to help.

She lowered herself to the child's eye level, smiling encouragement. "Isn't this neat, Timmy? This is your daddy's brother. They used to be little boys together. They lived in the same house, used to play games with each other...."

Apparently Timmy wasn't impressed. "Buddy wants to stay here," he said, inching closer to Suzanna.

Logan frowned. "Buddy?" he asked the boy.

Timmy slid around Suzanna's back until he was peering at Logan over her shoulder. He didn't answer.

"Buddy is Timmy's new puppy, right, Tim? Tell Uncle Logan what Buddy did this morning?"

Timmy's tiny chin dug into her shoulder, the breath from his open mouth warming her neck. The silence lengthened.

Abruptly Logan stood up. "Maybe we should continue this later."

Suzanna shot him a dark look. "He would have opened up, given a little more time. Some things can't be rushed."

Logan thrust a hand through his hair impatiently. But when he only nodded and said "Okay," she realized his impatience was directed at himself.

"So, where's this new puppy of yours, Tim?" he asked.

Timmy brightened. "In the bafroom."

"In the bafroom, eh? Well, let's go take a look." Logan smiled, and the smile transformed his face. Suzanna stared at him, bedazzled.

Timmy ran ahead of them and opened the bathroom door. "Uh-oh. He wet the floor again, Auntie Sue." The boy flopped onto his knees and, wrapping his arms around the pup's neck, squeezed him tight. The pup's back end waggled with matching enthusiasm.

Beside her, Logan snorted. "Good Lord, what is it?"

"What do you mean what is it?" Suzanna folded her arms.

"What breed?"

"He's . . . he's a cocker spaniel."

Logan cast her a look that made her squirm. "And where, pray tell, did you purchase this cocker spaniel?"

She felt heat rising up her face, but she lifted her chin nonetheless. "The Animal Rescue League." As Logan's eyebrow arched higher, her color deepened. "All right," she admitted. "He's a mixed breed, but so what! Mongrels are always smarter than purebreds. Everyone knows that."

Logan leaned against the doorjamb, arms crossed. She glanced away but could still feel his gaze moving over her, from her small pearl earrings to the hem of her summery yellow skirt. She was appalled to realize that the feeling wasn't altogether unpleasant.

"And am I to understand that this mongrel is coming with us?"

"Yes."

"We already have lots of dogs out at Mattashaum."

"Good, now you have one more. And I mean that. Timmy doesn't leave this house without him."

Logan made a low growling sound deep in his throat, but she noticed again that he was smiling, even if just a little.

"I still have some of Timmy's clothes to pack. Would you mind helping? You, too, Timmy. You can bring Buddy along."

Suzanna led the way into her nephew's bedroom. Hooking her foot under a small stool, she pulled it toward the bureau.

"What do you think you'll need from this drawer, Timmy?"

He clambered up and peeked in. "Pants?"

"Okay, pick out some pants." She wanted Timmy to be as involved with this move as possible. The last thing she wanted was for him to think she was forcing him out.

Meanwhile, Logan was tallying up the number of bags already packed. "Is all this really necessary? His nanny is perfectly capable of buying him new clothes. In fact, we were assuming she would."

"Yes, it is necessary." She glared over Timmy's head. The child needed to take as many familiar things as possible.

Logan only returned a look of exasperation and began to pace.

"Here, make yourself useful. Carry this bag down to your car."

By the time he returned she was almost done. "Just a few more items," she called from the closet. "Logan, would you put Buddy in his pet carrier, please?" She picked through a half-dozen pairs of shoes, and when she'd sorted the wearable ones from those that no longer fit, she turned around, expecting to see Logan struggling with a caramel-colored mop of fur.

Instead, she was surprised to find him staring down at something on the boy's nightstand. From the stillness of his shirt, he didn't appear even to be breathing.

Suzanna bit her lip when she realized what he was staring at—a photograph of Harris and Claudia. They were sitting on the floor in front of their first Christmas tree, Claudia quite obviously pregnant. It was Timmy's favorite picture, though why it was Suzanna wasn't certain. The festive tree perhaps, reminding him of his favorite time of year? The look of love and happiness in his young parents' eyes? Or the fact that he was in the picture, too, "hiding in Mommy's belly."

Logan picked up the frame, and even from a distance, she saw his shirt quiver with his indrawn breath.

Who are you, Logan Bradford? she wondered. *And why do you keep doing things that make it so hard for me to dislike you?*

Suddenly he turned and noticed her watching him. His expression immediately hardened, and he scooped up a stuffed animal from the bed and the pajamas Timmy had worn the previous night.

"These going, too?" he asked gruffly.

"Yes." She looked away and fussed with the few remaining items on the bureau, fighting back a smile.

By three-thirty everything had been put into the long black car—toys, clothing and a pet carrier that housed a very excited puppy. Logan was strapping Timmy into the middle of the front seat when Suzanna remembered she hadn't locked her door.

"Could you hold on a sec?" She jangled her house keys, and Logan nodded his understanding.

She ran up the walk and up the steps to the porch, trying not to think about the journey that lay ahead of her. Every instinct she possessed was still telling her this move was wrong. Yet what could she do? A judge had handed down a ruling, and the car was packed. The only thing now was to muddle through with whatever strength she could muster. "For Timmy's sake," she whispered as she opened the entry door.

With keys poised in front of the kitchen-door lock, however, a wave of sadness overtook her, a despair so profound she suddenly felt paralyzed by it. "Oh, Claudia, I let you down."

She'd thought she was alone until she heard Logan clear his throat. Quickly she lifted her head, tried to blink back tears and thrust the key toward the lock. She missed.

"Here, let me get that."

"I can manage," she said. He took the keys from her, anyway.

He locked the door, then paused, frowning down at her. Quite unexpectedly he said, "Don't worry. It'll be all right."

She was sure he meant nothing by that. They were merely words, the sort people always used to extricate themselves from uncomfortable situations. Yet she was so tired of shouldering problems alone that to have someone say, "Don't worry. It'll be all right," touched her to a degree that made no logical sense. Even though those words came from a sworn enemy, at this particular moment they sounded so comforting she felt her composure slide. With a sob that came from the deepest part of her, she buried her face in Logan's shirtfront.

Even as she was doing it she knew it was absurd. But just for this isolated moment she needed someone—and he was there.

His body felt stiff and restrained, his breathing shallow, and she supposed he was thinking about the absurdity of the moment himself. Still, when she drew in a long quivery breath, she felt a hand touch her hair, at first so light she almost missed it, then again, stroking this time.

"Shh, shh," he said.

Self-consciousness streamed through her, and she stepped away from his embrace. "I'm sorry," she said, trying to gather her dignity along with her composure. "This is embarrassing. It's just that I'm tired and worried. Please, Logan, you will take good care of him, won't you?"

He looked aside, his mouth tight, and she felt him withdrawing. "Of course. He's going to get the best of care."

He didn't really know what sort of responsibility he was assuming. He thought he did. He thought he knew everything. Yet she accepted his answer without further questions. That was the only way she could go on.

They drove out of the neighborhood and picked up the highway leading south. Soon the city fell behind them, its huge granite mills and ubiquitous church spires, its featureless high rises for the elderly, and then on the fringes, its newer shopping malls. The highway carried them away until finally there was nothing much to see but woods. A suburban town lay in scattered subdivisions, though only occasionally did they actually see a house. They played the radio and tried to talk about the music and news they heard. All the while little Timmy sat between them, his head swiveling with curiosity, his eyes overly wide with apprehension.

A sign announced their passage into another town, and Suzanna began to feel queasy. She knew this was the coastal town where Mattashaum was situated, and sure enough, Logan took the next exit.

The narrow country road they turned down meandered past farmlands and woods, somnolent under the high afternoon sun, around a shallow millpond where ducks squawked and slapped about the mud, then on through a village center that time had forgotten. At a playing field where four boys were attempting a game of baseball, Logan pulled into yet another long lane.

Suzanna checked her watch. They'd been driving for thirty-five minutes already. To Timmy it must seem an eternity, the miles between home and here immeasurable.

And then it was upon them—the entrance to Mattashaum. Suzanna found it a surprisingly simple entrance: two granite pillars about four feet high with the word "Mattashaum" chiseled into one and "Harbor" chiseled into the other. No gates barred the way, and an ordinary rural mailbox stood by the road. Old money, she surmised, needed to impress no one.

The driveway was narrow and snaked through a thick overhanging woods. Suzanna peered out the windshield in ever growing curiosity. Harris hadn't talked about Mattashaum much, only to say the house was a drafty colonial mausoleum near the ocean. Right now she couldn't see any sign of either house or ocean.

But she felt a definite sense of the ocean approaching. The trees were thinning, the sky was brightening with reflected light, and the air smelled salty and moist.

After what she gauged was nearly a mile, the woods fell away altogether—and the entire world opened out! Suzanna gaped in amazement while Logan let the car idle at the end of the paved road. Ahead of them, but still at quite a distance, was the most beautiful beach she'd ever beheld.

She squinted against the bright sunlight, taking, in a comprehensive sweep, the lay of the land. The beach curved inward in a gentle crescent, perhaps ten or twelve miles long, the two tips of that crescent thickly dotted with substantial Victorian seaside homes. It occurred to her that the party she'd catered two and a half years earlier had been out on one of those points. But of course she'd approached from an entirely different route.

Her gaze retracted, pulling back to grassy dunes, broad swaths of sea meadow, scrub growth and inland ponds.

"Well, what do you think?" Logan asked, his eyes alight with pride.

"I—I'm a little lost," she admitted. "Where exactly is Mattashaum?"

He hooked his wrists over the steering wheel and turned a smile on her. "Why, this is all Mattashaum."

Her eyes rounded. "Holy..."

Timmy scrabbled out of his safety belt and knelt up on the seat. "Holy," he repeated, imitating her.

"When this country was first being settled, land was pretty easy to come by, and land along water like this was considered almost useless. We had more than enough tillable acreage, though, and we made a killing raising beef cattle. Later, mid-1800s, we turned to dairy cows. All that area there—" he pointed to meadows on the right "—was used for pasture."

Suzanna was still trying to take it in when Logan set the car in motion again, turning left up a driveway.

"And this," he announced, "is the house."

Unlike the weathered, cedar-shingled summer homes on the points, the Bradford house was sheathed in clapboard and painted white, with neat black shutters at each of its multipaned windows. Its lines were simple and classic, no Queen Anne turrets here, no frivolous gables or fanciful gingerbread.

"The original house was built in 1710. That's the wing you see facing us. But over the years it's been added to considerably."

The house sat atop a slight rise in the land, a pair of two-storied wings fitted to each other at right angles. Enormous maples cast deep shade over its broad lawns, while two tall lilac bushes guarded the front door, looking as rooted in time as the house itself.

Logan parked near the door and they all piled out. The air was still and warm and rang with the sibilance of cicadas. From this vantage point, the house commanded an even more impressive view of the beach. Suzanna turned, shading her eyes. So much to see, so much to take in. Suddenly her heart sank with despair.

The Bradfords owned a little piece of heaven, and if all she had to pit against them was her love and a three-decker tenement house, then winning Timmy back was going to be the battle of her life.

CHAPTER FIVE

COMING IN from the bright sunlight, Logan removed his sunglasses. The house was always cool, even in summer, and with the green canvas shades three-quarters drawn, always dark.

"Auntie Sue, where are you?" Timmy whimpered.

"Right here, love."

Logan watched Suzanna place her hands on the boy's shoulders. "I can't see, either," she said. "That happens sometimes when you come into a house from very bright sunlight."

Logan tried to suppress a smile. She was blinking like an owl, totally unaware that he was staring at her. Unaware, too, of how pretty she looked, in a confused vulnerable sort of way.

But then, she *was* vulnerable, and Logan was feeling a protectiveness toward her and the boy he wouldn't have anticipated in a million years. The boy he could understand. But Suzanna? It wasn't natural.

"So, she came, after all," his father's voice grated from the shadows at the end of the hall.

Logan's right hand drifted to Timmy's head, his left hand to Suzanna's shoulder. "Hello, Collin. Of course she came. You knew she would." He tried to modulate his voice to conceal the fact that he and Collin had argued this issue all morning. Maybe his father was right and Timmy *would* be better off making a clean break, but Logan wasn't about to ignore a court order. Defiance would only jeopardize his chance of winning permanent custody.

He gazed at Timmy and his pulse accelerated. He still couldn't get over the emotional punch he'd felt on seeing this child for the first time, this cherub who looked so much like Harris at four. He hadn't been prepared. Until that moment Timmy had just been an idea to Logan, a responsibility, a case to win, a gift to Collin. But now he understood Judge Slade's words about dealing with a person, a tiny human being, and he could hardly wait for Collin to meet him.

The old man strode forward, tall, erect, his walking stick swinging and thumping the wide pineboard floor with a regular beat. He stopped a couple of feet in front of Suzanna, two hands fisted atop the stick. Logan waited for him to look at Timmy, his breath shallow with anticipation. Instead, Collin's eyes remained fixed on Suzanna.

"I don't know why you came, missy." His words fell like small chips of ice. "You aren't needed here."

Logan saw Suzanna stiffen. "Nor wanted, either," she replied. "But I am here, and I plan to stay until I feel assured Tim is comfortable."

Logan admired her pluck. His father's glare used to make his own knees knock when he was a boy, but she returned Collin's stare straightforwardly until finally he dismissed her with a disdainful sniff and turned his attention to the boy.

"Well, let's see him then. Is this our Timothy?" Before Logan realized what he was doing, Collin raised his stick and prodded the child on the leg.

Logan was sure the tap was feather-light, but Timmy let out a tiny cry nonetheless. He jumped behind Suzanna and buried himself in her skirt.

"Skittish little thing, isn't he?" Collin said, leaning on his stick again.

Logan was so appalled he couldn't move and was all the more amazed, therefore, when Suzanna knelt down and had the magnanimity to say, "It's okay, Tim. That's only your grandfather. Remember your daddy? Well, that's *his* daddy."

At the reference to Harris, Logan felt a sudden constriction in his chest. He looked at his father, searching for a kindred emotion, but Collin's face was as blank as a wiped slate. Logan thrust his hand through his hair, feeling increasingly confused.

Eyes wide and watery, Timmy looked up at his grandfather.

"Go say hello," Suzanna encouraged.

Timmy took a tentative step away from her, and then another. Collin leaned over and in his typically crusty manner said, "Hello, Timothy." Immediately Timmy ran back and threw his arms around his aunt.

Logan's lungs seemed to swell and burn with frustration. Timmy had been doing so well in the car. Logan had even got him to laugh a few times. But meeting Collin was wiping out whatever progress he'd made.

Ah, well. He supposed that was only to be expected. Every time Timmy met someone new, he was bound to withdraw a little. But he'd adjust. He would. Isn't that what everybody had been saying since this fiasco began?

"May I see Timmy's room, please?" Suzanna asked. Logan noticed her voice trembled.

Collin began to protest. "I don't see any point—"

"Yes, of course." Logan shot his father a sharp look. "But first, what do you say we let Buddy out of the car?" Logan wasn't ready for the sudden smile the boy blessed him with—or for the melting sensation he experienced in the region of his chest.

Collin followed them outside, and when the puppy leapt from the back seat, he let out a strangled "Egad!"

"That's your grandson's dog," Suzanna informed him, leaving no room for argument.

Logan tried to hide his grin. There were five dogs on the property already, all of them purebred retrievers or collies.

Collin's color deepened. "Logan, make sure to run this mutt over to the vet for shots and defleaing first thing tomorrow. We shouldn't allow him in the kennel with the other dogs yet."

Suzanna's spine straightened. "Buddy does not have fleas, I've already started him on his shots, and what's this business about a kennel?" Instead of addressing Collin, however, Suzanna turned her big green eyes on Logan.

He swallowed. "Apparently Timothy is quite attached to the dog," he explained to Collin. "Miss Keating kept him in her apartment, and the boy fell into the habit of sleeping with him."

Collin stared as if his son had lost his mind. Dogs had never been allowed in their house, and certainly never in anyone's bed.

"We'll talk about this later," he said.

Meanwhile Timmy was tumbling on the lawn with his pet.

"Well, see there?" Collin waved. "He's feeling at home already, Miss Keating. I'll arrange for someone to return you to the city."

"Collin, I think she'd like to meet the nanny and see the place first—you know, be assured of the boy's care?"

His father cocked his head. "She doubts the quality of the boy's care? *She* doubts...?"

Logan counted to ten. "It's her right," he finally answered calmly. Suzanna cast him a look of surprise laced with gratitude.

"Fine," Collin answered crisply. "Fine. Shall we start with the grounds then?"

He walked with angry determination, showing Suzanna the estate. At times she almost had to run to keep up. Logan gave up trying to slow him down and resorted to carrying Timmy on his shoulders.

Collin marched them around the pool, through the gardens and into the garage. He showed her the dry-docked sailboat and the barns that used to be part of the farm.

By the time they reached the stable, Logan was fairly angry himself. Collin was gloating. There was no other way to interpret it. Gloating over everything he could provide Timmy, and Suzanna couldn't.

Logan had pictured the afternoon much differently, too—a momentous meeting of grandson and grandfather and the beginning of a healing process, both physical and emotional. But Collin had turned it into a contest, with Timmy merely the prize to be won.

"Timothy," Collin barked, approaching a stall. "Do you like this pony? He's yours, you know. I bought him just for you. Come here, son."

Standing apart, Logan pressed a hand to his neck, disturbed by his father's behavior, yet not knowing what he could do about it. Not knowing if he should do anything. It wouldn't be wise to give the impression there was dissention between the two of them, especially when there really wasn't any.

In his peripheral vision, Logan saw Suzanna shoot him an alarmed look. Damn! Why was she continually turning to *him?* When had he become her ally, the solution to her problems?

Timmy approached the pony with caution. Suzanna opened her mouth, covered it with two hands, teetered on the edge of uncertainty, and then blurted, "Wait! He's only four years old!"

Collin pinned her with his contemptuous stare. "Miss Keating, that child's father was riding like a jockey by the time he was four."

Silently Logan swore. Yes, Harris had been riding—and hating every minute of it.

Just then the pony whinnied and Timmy jumped back in alarm. He turned and bolted for Suzanna, but before he reached her Collin caught him up, dangling him at arm's length.

"What, a Bradford afraid of a horse! We've rescued this child none too soon, Logan."

Struggling against his grandfather's firm hold, Timmy looked ready to cry. Suzanna's resentment radiated off her in palpable waves.

"Put him down," she demanded. "Right now."

With a sneer, Collin complied, and Suzanna held out her arms. But instead of going to her, a confused hurt look entered Timmy's eyes, and he ran to his puppy, instead, burying his face in the dog's silky coat. Logan saw Suzanna's face fall, and unexpectedly he ached for her.

"Can we go back to the house now?" she pleaded, again turning those soulful eyes on him. "All this—it's too much for Timmy all at once. Can we see his room and settle him in?"

Collin smiled with satisfaction. "But of course," he answered.

Inside the foyer, Collin announced that he was going to take his afternoon nap, a daily predinner habit since his heart attack. Logan tried not to feel resentful, but he hadn't expected this today. For weeks, his father had talked of nothing but bringing the boy home. Now he was here—and Collin was going to take a nap?

"Where's that nanny we hired?" Logan inquired. "I think Miss Keating would like to meet her."

Collin hummed and blustered. "She'll be here tomorrow. Something came up. I really must go and get some rest. See you at dinner." He paused on the stairs and turned to address Suzanna. "I trust you'll be gone by the time I arise, so I'll say goodbye to you now." Then he continued on his way.

Logan stared disbelievingly at his father's tall retreating figure, then glanced from Suzanna to Timmy, feeling caught in the middle of a problem he'd never meant to create. Not that he didn't take responsibility. Although Collin had come up with the idea of seeking guardianship, he had fallen right in with it. Damn! When would he ever learn?

Logan gave his head a shake. He really shouldn't let the situation get to him. This was only Timmy's first day here, and probably the worst. He was bound to settle in after today, and Collin's behavior would undoubtedly become more balanced, too. Things would work out. They would. They had to.

"Come on. I'll show you Timmy's room."

SUZANNA FOLLOWED Logan up the stairs, hating him, hating Collin, hating even this house. It was dark and formal and overwhelmingly masculine, with a preponderance of leather and brass and paintings of fox hunts and ancestors who glowered down their aristocratic Bradford noses at her as she climbed the stairs.

"This is your room, Tim," Logan said, opening a door at the end of the hall. "It used to be your father's."

Timmy peeked in warily. The room was tasteful enough, but like the rest of the house, not meant for a child. It was furnished in dark antiques, with lots of hunter-green plaids and sophisticated paisleys. Suzanna tried to say something encouraging, but her throat closed up on her.

"And my room is right through here, Tim, through this connecting door. It can be our secret passage, okay?"

"Okay." Timmy's voice was small and uncertain and nearly broke Suzanna's heart.

"Shall we unpack your toys first?"

The child nodded, and within an hour they had all his things transferred to drawers or closets or bookshelves. Suzanna noticed that the photograph of Harris and Claudia had somehow appeared on the nightstand, too.

She was propping Timmy's favorite stuffed animals on the bed when a voice called through an intercom that dinner was almost ready.

"That's our housekeeper, Mrs. Travis," Logan informed her. "I'll introduce you when we go down."

Suzanna hesitated. "Do you mind if I stay?"

"Not at all. Don't pay too much attention to what my father says. We . . . I expected you to stay."

She refused to thank him, although the urge was there.

"Logan?" Her brow tightened. "I have a favor to ask."

He turned to look at her from the doorway. She started to lose courage. "Go on," he urged.

"Will you please remember that *you* are Timmy's guardian?" He looked perplexed until she added, "And Collin isn't."

A muscle in his cheek jumped. "Let's not keep Mrs. Travis waiting."

Dinner was a disaster. The room was too formal, and the food dry and tasteless. Combined with Collin's acerbity, Suzanna found she could barely eat. And Timmy, poor child, had his head tucked under the tablecloth for most of the meal.

But the topper of the evening came in the form of Buddy wetting on the carpet. A genuine antique Oriental carpet, no less.

"Mrs. Travis, come in here." Collin's voice trembled with controlled anger.

The kindly faced housekeeper appeared in the doorway. "Yes, Mr. B.?"

"Get this mutt out of here. Take him to the kennel. Now!"

Timmy popped up from under the table in alarm. "No, don't take Buddy." His eyes finally filled with the tears he'd bravely suppressed all day.

The housekeeper hesitated, glancing from Collin to the boy.

"Take him!" Collin snapped.

Suzanna looked to Logan, but he just turned his head. She swallowed her disappointment and called herself a fool

for thinking he might intervene. She had no allies in this
house and didn't understand why she'd started to think she
had.

"It's best, Tim," she said calmly. "Until Buddy's trained,
he really belongs outside. He'll be fine. He's just going to
meet the other dogs and make friends."

"Oh." The child picked up his fork, but he only moved
the food around on his plate.

Suzanna and Logan took him up to his room soon after.
Sitting on one side of the bed, Suzanna stroked Timmy's
light brown hair, helping him surrender to his exhaustion.
When he was asleep, she finally let her gaze lift to Logan,
sitting on the other side. He was watching her with an in-
tentness that made her terribly self-conscious.

"I'll be by as soon as possible tomorrow," she said. "I
have some things I have to do at the shop in the morning."

"Don't rush. The nanny will be here...and so will I."
Logan sighed in resignation. "I'll stay home from work tomorrow."

Somehow, Suzanna hadn't pictured Logan working. At
least not going off to a job. And she wondered, what *had*
she thought he did with his time?

She licked her parched lips and noticed him follow the
gesture with his eyes. Quickly she rose from the bed, feeling increasingly confused.

"You will keep the connecting door open, won't you?"

"Yes. And I'll be sure to have Mrs. Travis prepare pancakes for his breakfast."

"With strawberry syrup, if she has any. And if he wets the
bed..."

"Don't worry. He's going to be fine."

She nodded, and before tears had a chance to surface, she
dashed from the room.

Yes, Timmy was going to be fine, she assured herself as
the housekeeper's husband drove her home through the
dark and empty night. He was sleeping soundly in the

beautiful antique sleigh bed that used to be his father's. He was dreaming to the soothing lullaby of the sea. He had a nanny, a pony, a twenty-room house....

Suzanna buried her face in her hands, muffling what might've been a sob.

Timmy had everything money could buy. The only thing he didn't have was love.

AT TWO-FIFTEEN Logan awoke. He lay very still and alert, but the only sound he heard was the sea's incessant murmur in the distance beyond his open window. Then it came again—a soft muffled sob.

Logan threw back the sheets, switched on his bedside lamp and stumbled toward the connecting door.

"What's up, pal?" Logan sat on the edge of the bed. Timmy was burrowed somewhere under the covers. He placed his hand on the small warm mound and discovered it was shivering. "Hey, it's all right. I'm here." But Timmy just burrowed deeper. Apparently he didn't care that Logan was there. Suzanna wasn't, and it was becoming more and more evident that that was all that mattered.

Slowly Logan eased back the covers and lifted the child onto his lap. His hair was matted, his pajamas damp with perspiration. Dear Lord, Logan thought, how long had this child been awake and cowering in the dark before making a noise?

"Were you having a bad dream?" Logan stroked Timmy's arm. "I have bad dreams sometimes, too. It's okay. They're not real."

Timmy looked around the room, his eyes glazed and blank. It was a room to which Logan had not given much consideration until now. How unlike the cheerful room Timmy had left behind in Suzanna's apartment, with its race-car bed and fanciful mobiles and cartoon characters dancing across a field of white wallpaper.

Logan scooped Timmy up and paced the room, jiggling him in what he hoped was a comforting fashion. "It's okay, Tim," he crooned. "Everything's fine. I'm here. I'm not going to leave you."

After several minutes of pacing and soft assurances, Timmy's rigid limbs began to relax. Nestling into Logan's shoulder, he reached up and idly played with Logan's ear. Finally Logan thought he heard him speak.

"What did you say, Tim?"

The answer was muffled into the hollow of Logan's shoulder, yet he understood.

"Buddy? Why, he's down in the kennel with his new friends. Right now he's probably fast asleep dreaming about big bowls of kibbles."

"But he's afraid." Timmy lifted his head and pinned Logan with his irresistible blue eyes. "He doesn't like to sleep alone. He cries."

Logan scowled, sadness overtaking him without warning. "Does he really? Well, we'll just have to bring him upstairs with us where he'll feel better, won't we?"

Against his chest, Logan felt a trembling laugh of relief, and something inside him turned over. Judge Slade had used the word "fragile" to describe Timmy's condition. How little Logan had understood what he'd meant.

With Timmy in his arms, Logan tiptoed down the dimly lit hall past his father's room, quietly descended the stairs and slipped out the door.

At the first serious spate of barking, Logan flipped on the light inside the kennel to let the dogs see who their intruder was. The yipping stopped almost immediately, followed by a sudden alertness and a wagging of tails.

"There he is!" Timmy's eyes, tired as they were, filled with delight.

Yawning, Logan unlocked the cage and, shifting Timmy to one arm, scooped Buddy up into the other. The pup squirmed excitedly and licked everything he could reach, including Logan's chin. Logan was surprised to find himself chuckling.

As stealthily as they'd left the house they reentered it, detouring through the kitchen for milk and cookies before heading up the stairs. Logan found a storybook in Timmy's room, and soon all three were settled into Logan's bed, snuggled into a plump nest of pillows. Then in a low soothing voice, Logan read the adventure to the child and the pup who were tucked under his arm. Both were becoming increasingly placid with each page, their breathing slower and more regular.

Finally Logan looked down and saw that both were asleep. He lay the book aside, whispering, "And they lived happily ever after." He smiled softly. So much warmth there. So much vulnerability. He sighed, resting his head back on the pillows, and closed his bleary eyes.

How much this little boy reminded him of Harris at four. They were nearly carbon copies. Similarly, how often had Harris ended up here in Logan's bed, especially during that frightening time right after their mother left. Six years older, Logan hadn't had a chance to indulge his own fears or insecurities. He'd had to play the comforting big brother right from the start.

Now it was happening all over again. Logan tipped his head forward and rested his lips on the boy's warm head. He was beginning to think Collin had made a mistake in deciding to bring Timmy home so abruptly. And Logan had made a worse mistake in aiding and abetting that decision.

Ah, well, the die had been cast, and he couldn't turn back now. What he could do, however, was make certain that Suzanna spent as much time as possible here at Mattashaum to help the boy settle in. The thought brought an unbidden smile to Logan's lips, a smile he promptly banished.

That would be a tricky situation, though. She was bound to become suspicious if he suddenly rolled out the red carpet, and the last thing he wanted was her realizing that Timmy was having difficulties.

Pride accounted for much of this attitude; he'd boasted how much better off the child would be under his care, and he'd truly believed he was right. But another part of him feared that Suzanna might use the situation against him in court. No, what he had to do was make sure she spent sufficient time here with Timmy and yet keep her from finding out how much she was needed.

Of course, there was another alternative: give Timmy up. But already Logan knew he couldn't do that. He sank into the pillows, letting the air seep slowly from his lungs, letting his thoughts drift back....

He'd been wrong to stop speaking to Harris. Even though concern for Collin had led him into making that decision, he'd still been wrong. All those lost years—and for what? Logan didn't even know anymore.

He shook his head sadly. He'd been so sure there would be time enough for them to make up, so sure he'd see his brother again....

No, he couldn't give up Timmy now that he'd met him. Although time had run out before he could do anything about Harris, maybe through Harris's son he could still atone.

Logan eased his arm from under his warm sleeping burden and turned off the light. But it was a long while before he was able to sleep.

CHAPTER SIX

SUZANNA'S EIGHT-YEAR-OLD van rattled down the Bradfords' private roadway early the next afternoon, drawing attention to the fact that she needed new shocks. But new shocks were hardly a concern at the moment. Reaching Timmy was.

She'd called that morning at eight o'clock—early, she knew, but she couldn't restrain herself any longer. She'd missed her nephew so much and worried herself almost sick wondering how he'd fared through the night.

But Logan had answered the phone and assured her that everything was fine. Timmy had slept like a log, was eating a big plate of pancakes with strawberry syrup and looking forward to a morning of play with his nanny who'd just arrived. He'd also said that a crew was there unloading lumber for a swing set. Could she hear the racket they were making? Timmy was pretty excited about that, too. There was really no reason for her to rush out to Mattashaum, he'd said. If she felt she absolutely had to come, then a short visit after lunch would do.

By the time Suzanna had hung up, she'd felt thoroughly deflated. Maybe the Bradfords were right, after all; Timmy was young and would adjust to living with them with no problem. Maybe he really didn't need her.

She should be happy. She didn't want her nephew to suffer nightmares or separation anxiety, right?

But how could she be happy, when his adjusting meant she was losing him?

Luckily her morning had become so busy she'd hardly had time to think about Timmy again until lunchtime. She had several large pickup orders to prepare and a fiftieth-anniversary party for two hundred guests coming up on Sunday. And, just to add a little mayhem where none was needed, the bathroom pipes on the third floor developed another leak. Now, Suzanna felt as worn out as her shocks.

She came to the end of the paved lane and turned left up the driveway to the house. Even from a distance, she could feel its coldness reaching toward her.

Mrs. Travis answered the door. She was a pleasant quiet-spoken person with kind eyes and a warm smile. She lived over the garage with her caretaker husband.

"Your nephew is out back with his uncle and the new nanny. Come take the shortcut through the house."

"They're expecting me, aren't they?"

"Oh, yes," the woman said, rolling her eyes. Suzanna frowned, wondering what she meant, but Mrs. Travis pushed on without further comment.

Suzanna glanced into the dining room where she'd eaten last evening, the brass chandelier winking bravely despite the drawn shades. The housekeeper ushered her through the sitting room and opened a French door.

"Courage," she whispered, giving Suzanna's arm a squeeze.

Suzanna smiled her thanks, then stepped out onto a flag-stone patio. Beyond the patio, in the shade of a huge spreading maple, Timmy was sitting on a blanket, listlessly petting his puppy who lay by his side.

Over the phone this morning, Logan had claimed the boy was doing fine; he'd even implied he was thriving. But obviously Timmy was *not* fine. He looked pale and tired, and Suzanna's heart ached with sorrow and helplessness.

A few feet to Timmy's right, a strapping dark-haired woman of about forty sat in an Adirondack chair reading a magazine. A few feet to his left, like a matching sconce, sat

Logan Bradford reading a book. Beside him was a table set up with a vase of wildflowers and a pitcher of lemonade. They seemed a tableau, carefully arranged to present an idyllic summer afternoon. Only trouble was, Suzanna saw through their charade.

As if on cue, all three looked up.

"Auntie Sue!" Timmy cried, breaking into a smile. He scrambled to his feet and came running toward her.

She picked him up and gave him a tight hug. "Hey, kiddo," she choked out, tears burning in her throat.

"Where *were* you?" he cried, his voice hurt and accusing.

"I..." She wasn't sure she knew how to answer him, and so merely finished in a whisper, "I love you, babe."

She set him down and took his hand. Both Logan and the nanny had risen from their chairs and were checking her out, their eyes moving slowly in judgmental appraisal. She'd brushed her hair back and tied it neatly with ribbon and had chosen a simple pink shirtwaist to wear. She didn't think she offered anything to gawk at.

"Good afternoon," she said crisply.

"Miss Keating." Logan Bradford nodded, his gray eyes traveling from her hair to her shoes. In spite of her resentment, Suzanna felt her cheeks warm.

"This is Trudi Barrows, Timmy's nanny," he continued. "Trudi, Suzanna Keating, Timmy's aunt."

Normally Suzanna didn't judge people by appearances, which was why she was having such difficulty with her negative reaction to Trudi Barrows now. But everything about the woman was big. Big teeth, big ears, lantern jaw. Even her eyes popped out, making Suzanna wonder guiltily if the poor woman had a thyroid condition. Suzanna felt thoroughly ashamed of herself, but heavens, it was the sort of face that might easily give a child nightmares. She flashed Trudi a brief smile in atonement.

"Have a seat," Logan said, gesturing toward a chair next to his. "Would you like some lemonade?"

"No, thank you."

They all sat and avoided looking at each other. Tension thickened the air. Suzanna wondered if this was to be her visit, if she was supposed to just sit here and chat. It wasn't what she'd envisioned. She'd hoped for a few hours alone with her nephew, playing in his room or wandering the grounds. She hadn't counted on being monitored and chaperoned.

Then again, if she wanted Timmy to feel comfortable with these people, perhaps she should show him that they were people she felt comfortable with, too.

Timmy crawled into her lap and immediately his thumb went into his mouth.

Suzanna turned to Trudi Barrows, smiling as pleasantly as she could under the circumstances. "Have you always worked as a nanny?"

"Oh, yes." Trudi smiled back, baring her startling teeth. "Since I was nineteen. I've lived all over the country—San Francisco, New York, Miami. My real ambition, though, is to get to Europe some day."

Suzanna tucked Timmy under her chin and felt her smile waver. "And you've never had the desire to have children of your own?"

"And give up my career?" The woman laughed, a honk that caused Buddy to lift his head and perk his floppy ears.

"Trudi is wonderful with children," Logan hastened to add. "She comes with the highest recommendations. Believe me, Timmy is getting the best of care. By the way, have you seen his new swing set?"

Suzanna was well aware that he'd switched subjects. Aware, too, of the lines of tiredness that bracketed his mouth.

"Is that it?"

"Yes. Isn't it something?"

It was something, all right. Out on the sunny lawn stood a structure that looked less like a swing set than a cottage-size redwood sculpture, although among the various platforms, ladders, ropes and slides, Suzanna did spy something that resembled a swing. She frowned, picturing her small fenced yard, its only diversion a simple sandbox.

"Come on, Timmy," his nanny urged, rising and holding out her hand. "Let's show your aunt how you can climb right to the top. Come on," she repeated more sternly when he didn't move.

"Go on, love," Suzanna encouraged, though her glance toward the nanny was cool.

Reluctantly he slid off her lap and Trudi took his hand. "He's a little tired now," she explained, "but that's just because we've been playing all morning."

Suzanna gave the woman's starched gray dress a cursory glance. If Timmy had been playing, it hadn't been with her.

"Whee!" Trudi said in her deep monotone, giving the swing a push. "Whee!" Timmy's mouth set into a tight downward curve.

No sooner had Trudi got the swing going than she stopped it and instructed Timmy to try the slide, and after the slide, she told him to climb the monkey bars.

Obediently he worked his way up, over and through all the various features of the elaborate structure until finally his nanny clapped her hands and said, "Wasn't that fun?"

Sensing his performance was over, Timmy popped his thumb back into his mouth and hurriedly returned to Suzanna's lap.

"And wasn't it nice of Uncle Logan to buy it for you?" a gruff voice called from the patio.

Timmy's small body stiffened at the sound of his grandfather's voice. Suzanna turned to find not only Collin walking toward them but also Cecily Knight, the blonde to whom Logan was engaged. A feeling of desperation rose in her. Timmy was obviously on the verge of tears. He was tired, unhappy and terribly confused by all these strangers. Suzanna held him to her, trying to think. There had to be a way out of this.

Instinctively her eyes lifted to Logan, though for the life of her she didn't know why she continued to turn to him. She was surprised to find a deep frown creasing his brow. He hadn't said anything while the nanny was putting Timmy through his paces trying to prove what a fun-filled place Mattashaum was, but Suzanna had noticed him sitting tensely, his fingers linked and thumbs circling each other as if an immense amount of nervous energy was concentrated in those two digits. Now his hands were still. Everything about him had stilled—except his eyes, which, under those fierce lowered brows, moved from face to face. Suzanna felt she was sitting beside a gathering thunderhead.

Cecily Knight sailed across the patio and swooped down on Timmy with an exuberant smile. He jerked back against Suzanna's breastbone, pressing away from the young woman who nonetheless managed to stamp his cheek with a bright lipstick kiss.

"Oh, he's adorable, Logan." The blonde stood back, clasping her hands under her chin in delight. Logan's mouth twitched in a semblance of a smile.

Cecily, dressed in a pristine tennis outfit and visor, got down on one knee in front of Suzanna and, donning an expression of sympathy, placed a hand on her arm. "And you're Suzanna." Her voice was low, her beautiful blue eyes full of solicitous commiseration. "I know this is a difficult time for you, but I want you to know I intend to be a very good mother to Timmy. I love children, so does Logan, and I can assure you Timmy will be raised in a very happy home."

The longer Cecily talked, the stiffer Timmy's body grew—and the harder Suzanna had to fight the urge to get up, carry him to her van and drive away. Did this woman think the child was deaf? Couldn't she see what she was doing—this stranger, this absolute stranger—with her talk of becoming his mother?

"Auntie Sue, we go home now, okay?" Timmy's voice wavered badly. Suzanna wrapped him closer, stroking his head.

"It's '*May* we go home now,'" his nanny brayed. "Can you say that, Timothy? May we?"

Suzanna thought she might scream. Legalities be damned! This arrangement was all wrong. There had to be a way of getting Timmy out of here. But what? Was there a court order she could procure? A child-rights group she could complain to?

She was still wrestling with her desperation when Logan shot to his feet and walked from the circle of chairs. He paused several feet away with his back to them, powerful shoulders high and tight, hands hooked tensely at his waist.

"Logan," his father cajoled, though his voice was spiked with steel. "Come sit with Cecily and tell Miss Keating about the trip to Walt Disney World the three of you plan to take next month."

Logan turned, and Suzanna was amazed by the anger she saw in his face. His eyes were fiery, his dark cheeks flushed, and his bloodless lips worked as if he longed to lash out. But he didn't. His chest merely rose and fell, rose and fell, until finally his agitation subsided somewhat.

"Suzanna," he said.

Her whole body responded with a small jump. He'd never called her by her first name before. "Y-yes?"

"I think Timmy would enjoy a walk down to the beach. What do you think?"

"Logan, sit down and—"

"I don't feel like sitting, Father." Though he spoke respectfully, his jaw was set hard, and his eyes remained fixed on Suzanna, speaking to her in a wordless message.

Her pulse beat with flurried excitement. "Yes. Yes, I think he'd love a walk."

With an exasperated huff, the nanny started to rise. "Just let me get my sweater—"

"No," Logan told her. "You've been on duty all day. Why don't you take a break now." And moving his angry gaze from Trudi to Cecily and then to his father, he added, "Why don't you all take a break." He spoke so commandingly that no one stirred.

After lifting Timmy from Suzanna's lap and propping him on one arm, Logan held out his free hand to her. Suzanna stared at it, at his surprisingly calloused palm, at his wide thumb, long fingers, clean blunt-filed nails. Several seconds passed. And then, feeling as if she was stepping into sheer space, she lay her own hand in his. It was warm, rough, strong, and when it closed around hers she felt an illogical sense of security. And something more. Partnership.

They walked away from the house in silence, knowing they were being watched, and not until they were far down the gravel path did their brisk pace ease up. When they reached the dunes, Logan paused to lower Timmy to the sand where the puppy, who'd trotted after them, welcomed the child with several excited leaps.

"Thank you," Suzanna said, but her words were mumbled. She wasn't sure it was wise to openly admit gratitude to, of all people, Logan Bradford.

"For what?" Logan turned his hardened face to the wind as if questioning the wisdom of admitting that he had done her, of all people, a favor. Such pride, she thought. On both sides.

"I, well, you know what I mean."

"Look, Suzanna, just because I snapped at those people back there—" Logan thrust his hand through his long windblown hair "—doesn't mean I've taken your side."

"Well, of course not. I know that. You were only doing what was best for..." She cast a meaningful glance in Timmy's direction.

"Exactly."

"Which is why I said thank you. I appreciate what you did. He wasn't having a good time."

Logan gazed at the horizon for a long while, eyes narrowed. "Do you blame him?" he finally muttered.

Suzanna blinked. "What?"

"Well, were *you* having a good time? I sure as hell wasn't."

Suzanna stared at his strong profile, speechless, fighting an urge to smile.

"In their defense," he continued, "they were probably just nervous and trying too hard. Come on, let's keep walking," he suggested.

Feeling more at ease but still somewhat dumbfounded, Suzanna resumed plodding up the sandy path by his side. Timmy, whose spirits also seemed to be perking, wedged himself between them and reached for their hands.

"So, where'd she come from?" Suzanna asked.

"She who?"

"Trudi Barrows, the nanny."

"Oh, you mean Brunhilda?"

Suzanna surprised herself by laughing and noticed a grin overtaking Logan's expression, too.

"Yes, her. Could you tell me what her credentials are?"

"I haven't the foggiest. She isn't the nanny I hired. The one I hired decided at the last minute not to take the post. I suspect she and my father may have argued. So Brunhilda showed up, instead."

"It isn't funny, Logan. So many new people, so much change."

The laugh lines faded from Logan's face, and suddenly she was sorry to see them go. "I know," he admitted.

Just then Timmy's sneaker caught in the sand and he started to stumble. Simultaneously both Suzanna and Logan lifted him by the hands they clasped. Arcing through the air, the little boy giggled, and when he landed, they swung him again.

Smiling, Suzanna glanced at Logan. Warmth softened his features. Quickly they both looked away.

"Is this okay with Cecily? Your leaving her to come for a walk?"

Logan looked baffled for a moment. "Oh, Cecily. No, this is fine. She doesn't mind."

"But it looked like she was coming to play tennis or something. Had you made plans?"

He swallowed, staring ahead. "No, none. This is fine."

Strange, Suzanna thought. She couldn't put her finger on it, but something was definitely strange about his and Cecily's relationship. He hadn't reacted at all when she'd arrived. No sudden smile, no leap of fire in his eyes. She kept her thoughts to herself, however, and turned her attention to her surroundings.

"What a beautiful day." She sighed, tipping back her head. Gliding across a perfectly blue sky, seabirds caught the sun on their outstretched wings. She breathed deeply of the tangy salt air, felt the tall swaying grasses prickle her legs, listened to the boom of the surf—and knew a sense of freedom that didn't really make sense.

"Yes, it is nice," Logan agreed, looking around as if in surprise.

They'd come over the dunes now and were standing at the top of the beach. Without any urging Timmy let go of their hands and scampered ahead with his pet.

"Are you comfortable walking in those things?" Logan inquired, prying off his topsiders.

Suzanna flattened her wind-billowed skirt and glanced down at her leather-soled white flats. "They do insist on filling with sand." She kicked them off and lay them alongside his. "Much better." She smiled up at him while wiggling her toes in the soft warm sand. This time when their eyes met, they held, and her stomach did a crazy tumble. Slowly they each looked away.

"It's too b-bad we didn't come prepared," Suzanna stammered as they continued their stroll toward the water. "No bathing suits. No suntan lotion. Not even a towel."

Logan squinted out at one of the points. "Maybe next time."

Next time? she thought. And would he be along, too?

At the high-tide mark, where seaweed and broken shells dried in a long dark line, Logan patiently removed Timmy's sneakers and socks. Suzanna couldn't help noticing how trusting Timmy was of him. With Logan, he showed none of the wariness he displayed with the others back at the house.

"Knowing Timmy," she said, "I think we should remove his shorts, too." She sat cross-legged on the sand, ready to help.

"That right? You think you might be going for a swim, pal?" Logan asked while rolling up his chinos.

"Swimmm!" Timmy sang, arching back so exuberantly he almost toppled over.

Logan laughed, and Suzanna's heart did a flip-flop.

She stood up hurriedly and brushed her skirt. She had to get a grip on reality. Logan Bradford was her adversary, a man who was trying to take Timmy away from her. He had caused Harris and her sister immeasurable heartache and financial difficulty. He'd insulted her by saying her motives for seeking guardianship were monetary. He was not someone whose laugh she should be finding so fascinating right now. Besides, he was engaged!

They walked across the smooth wet sand to the ocean's edge where Timmy stood as still as beached driftwood, not at all sure he liked the way the water rushed in and foamed around his ankles. When, after a few breakers had come and gone, he discovered his feet had sunk and disappeared, he let out a small alarmed cry.

Chuckling, Logan lifted him up, stepped into the water and swung him from side to side like a bell. Suzanna was relieved and then amazed to hear Timmy laughing while his feet skimmed the bubbling surf. A moment later, Logan had him calf deep, and finally Timmy was in up to his thighs. At that point Logan swung him back to the safe firmly packed sand where the child crowed with pride at his accomplishment.

"Let's take a walk down the beach, Tim, and see what we can see. Okay?" Logan spoke to the child, but he looked at Suzanna.

Again her cheeks warmed. Today, away from the house, Logan seemed different, the hard edges of his personality softening. Even his eyes seemed a warmer gray—and she found it increasingly difficult to remember why she should dislike him.

They came to a rocky area where big black boulders rose from the water and littered the lower beach, forming a kind of natural jetty. Logan squatted down by one of the rocks and called, "Come here, Tim. I want you to see something." He lifted aside a beard of seaweed to expose a colony of blue-black mollusks.

Eyes wide with curiosity, Timmy moved in close to his uncle. "What are them?"

"Them are what we call mussels, Tim."

"Muscles!" He giggled, flexing an imagined bicep.

"Not that kind, silly." Logan nudged the child with his knee, and again Suzanna was struck by how well they got along. Somehow, somewhere, these two had bonded.

"And those little round guys there, those are periwinkles." Logan pried one off the rock. "This is his house," he explained, tapping the shell. "And over here—see that little round scale, Tim?"

Suzanna leaned in, too.

"That's where Mr. Periwinkle lives, behind that door."

"Will he come out if we knock?" For the first time in days, Timmy seemed his old self—curious, happy, mindful only of the immediate moment.

"No, afraid not, Tim." Chuckling, Logan threw the periwinkle back, picked Timmy up and stepped between the rocks. "Got something else to show you," he said, and again he glanced back to see if Suzanna was following. She was.

He sat on a boulder and, holding Timmy firmly on one knee, leaned forward to peer at another rock, this one quite broad and shaped like a shallow bowl. By now his trousers were completely wet and sandy, clinging revealingly to his powerful legs, but he didn't seem to notice or to care. Suzanna surveyed her own clothing, found her skirt equally grubby, and with a careless shrug took a spot on an adjacent boulder.

"See these little guys, Tim," Logan said, pointing. "These are called barnacles."

"Where? In the puddle?"

"Uh-huh. We call a puddle like this a tide pool."

Suzanna's eyebrows lifted. Oh, so that was a tide pool.

"Look carefully, Tim."

The child leaned closer, as did Suzanna, strands of her hair blowing free, the wisps reflected in the still water. For a moment, Logan was quiet and she sensed he was watching her in the pool.

He cleared his throat. "See them moving, Tim?"

Suzanna gasped and cried, "Yes!"

He smiled up at her. "Those barnacles are tiny living animals, Tim, and what they're doing is eating."

"Eating?" the boy echoed.

"That's right. There are bits of food in the water so small we can't even see them."

For several minutes Timmy sat watching the barnacles feeding in the warm pool. And Suzanna sat watching Logan. She couldn't help it. He grew handsomer each time she saw him—and here on the beach he seemed to have entered his element. His straight dark hair shone with sunlight. His arms were brown and hard. Even his feet were beautifully shaped—the long bones, the graceful arch. They were tanned, too, an indication that he spent a great deal of time in the sun.

Suddenly she realized he was watching her, as well, his eyes traveling over her face, moving slowly, feature to feature—and finally stopping at the small beauty mark by her mouth. She felt her pulse race, her skin flush.

Quickly she gathered her skirt and got to her feet. "Sh-shall we keep walking, Timmy?"

Logan whistled and called for the puppy, who was engrossed in sniffing out invisible tracks through the dune grass, and they continued on their way.

A little farther down the beach they came upon what Logan called the creek, a narrow coursing waterway connecting the ocean with a calm inland pond. Twelve Acre Pond, Logan called it. They followed the creek's bank a short distance until they reached a place where the current and wind had deposited a swath of fine sand. There Logan invited Suzanna to sit while Timmy and his dog waded into the shallow stream.

"It's safe here," he said, "and he'll get lots of action. Schools of guppies, fiddler crabs..."

Suzanna shaded her eyes. "What do those say?" She pointed to a couple of small signs posted by the bushy vegetation on the other side of the creek.

"Oh, that area's a nesting ground for terns and plovers and a few other species who are having a hard time of it. That whole area's restricted."

"Really?" She straightened with deepened interest. "Do you get many people on your beach?"

"Enough. They walk down from the points."

"And do they obey the signs?"

Logan let out a long breath. "Most people are decent, but there are always a few who spoil it for the others. We used to open the beach to the public until three years ago. Lifeguards, bathhouses, the works."

"I didn't know that." Suzanna was beginning to realize there was a lot about Logan Bradford she didn't know.

"We charged a fee, of course. Made quite a profit on it, too. Believe me, closing wasn't easy. But it was necessary." He gazed up at a snow-white bird gliding on the breeze. "For a while, at least."

He went on to tell her about the shellfish in the pond and the osprey towers and erosion fences he maintained. But after a while Suzanna didn't hear the words. All she heard was the passion in his voice. Logan Bradford was apparently a committed environmentalist, and it didn't take much digging to discover why. He loved Mattashaum, loved it more than words could ever describe, and such an attachment mandated a sense of responsibility toward this fragile environment.

"Whose house is that out there?"

"What house?" Logan lay back, folding his hands behind his head.

"The cabinlike thing on the other side of the pond. Up the hill near the windmill."

He closed his eyes and was quiet for a moment. Meanwhile Timmy returned from playing in the creek and sat between them, yawning.

"That's...my place."

"Your place!"

"Mmm. I only use it occasionally," he hastened to add. "I built it mostly to test the windmill. I've been interested in alternate forms of energy, oh, almost all my life. My current obsession is windmills. I...own a factory that manufactures them, in fact."

"Really! That's fascinating." And noble, she thought. "But your cottage—surely it doesn't stay empty...."

Abruptly he got to his feet. "Timmy looks pretty tired, and it is getting on to dinnertime."

Suzanna rose, too, teeming with questions, but Logan was already lifting Timmy onto his shoulders. And so they retraced their steps, collecting scattered shoes and clothing on the way.

BY THE TIME they reached the house, Timmy was asleep. Logan had carried him all the way on his shoulders, and now he could feel the child's cheek lying heavily on his head.

"He's really out," Suzanna murmured. Logan watched her raise her hand and touch it gently to Timmy's back. They were standing on the now deserted patio, where they'd begun their afternoon adventure. She looked tired, and sad again, and reluctant to leave.

"I think I'll skip waking him for dinner," Logan said, "and just put him down for the night. What do you think?"

Suzanna frowned. "I doubt he'll sleep through."

Logan wished he hadn't ended their time on the beach so abruptly. She'd looked relaxed there. He was especially pleased that she'd come to see he wasn't quite the ogre she'd initially thought. As he'd talked about Mattashaum, he'd noticed real admiration in her eyes. He didn't know why that mattered to him, but it did.

But then she'd gone and mentioned the cottage, and for some reason he'd shut down.

"Logan?"

He liked hearing his name on her lips and savored the moment before answering. "Yes?"

"Would you mind very much if...if I took Timmy home with me tonight?"

Logan had been afraid this would happen. He wanted to stroke away the lines etched on her brow, wanted to see her smile again. She was so pretty when she smiled. But he didn't move, just stood facing her, his hands clasping Timmy's wrists, hoping she knew that he cared.

"I . . . don't think that would be wise, Suzanna."

Her lashes swept down to conceal her too-bright eyes. "But I know he's going to wake up, and I can't stay here any longer. Heaven knows I want to, but I still have a few hours of work to put in tonight." She chewed on her lower lip, the furrow in her brow deepening.

It couldn't be easy on her. She had a business to run, a house and tenants to see to.

Ignoring all the prudent voices that were telling him to hold still, Logan reached across the distance that separated them and tipped up her face so that she had to meet his eyes. "He'll be okay, I promise."

Was that the wrong thing to say? Suddenly a tear coursed down her cheek.

"You won't leave him to the care of . . . of anyone else?"

He knew she was thinking about the nanny and Collin and possibly even Cecily. "No. I won't leave him for a minute. He'll be fine."

Suzanna stepped away from his touch. "That's what you said yesterday."

"I know, but—"

She stilled him with a hand to his lips, an unexpected gesture that stole his breath. "What I'm trying to say is, this time I believe you. I don't know why, but I do. Please, Logan, don't let me down."

Still holding Timmy in place, Logan walked Suzanna around front to her van. "Are you coming by tomorrow? It probably isn't necessary—if you're falling behind in your work."

"I'll be by." She climbed into the van and gave Logan and Timmy one last look. He could tell her heart was aching at the thought of driving away.

"Trust me, Suzanna. I'll handle the situation."

She nodded, and before the tears that had welled up in her eyes had a chance to spill over, she flicked the ignition and drove off down the lane.

Long after she'd disappeared from sight, Logan remained standing on the driveway, lost in thought. He had a problem on his hands.

Damn! He'd tried to stick to the game plan and pretend that everything here at Mattashaum was fine, but finally he hadn't been able to take it anymore. *He'd* been the one walking the floor last night, not Collin. He'd been the one who'd wiped Timmy's tears and assured him his aunt would be back. Collin had slept through it all, as if throwing ponies and expensive swing sets at the child was all that was needed to make him happy.

Logan readjusted the warm placid weight in his arms, Suzanna's voice still whispering to him in the breeze, "Don't let me down." He gazed at the house where Collin was probably peeking from behind some heavy curtain, gazed past the house across the pond to where the westering sun cast its sweet golden light on a sweet golden hill.

He hadn't wanted to talk about the cottage because it wasn't just a place he'd built to test a windmill. The cottage was his escape—from Collin, from immutable memory, from areas of his life he couldn't possibly get into with Suzanna, lest she see all the ragged seams that held it together.

Logan looked again at the main house, looked back to the pond where a flock of gulls tilted into the gold of the sun, looked around to the lane down which Suzanna's van had just driven—and knew he had to make a decision. "Damn!" he whispered. He didn't need this. Didn't need this at all.

CHAPTER SEVEN

SUZANNA JERKED into fuzzy wakefulness and groped for her bedside phone. "H'lo?"

"Suzanna?"

"Logan?" Her eyes opened and her heart stilled.

"Sorry to be calling so early..."

She glanced at the clock. It was eight-fifteen. "No, no. I'm usually up by now. Is anything wrong?"

"On the contrary." She heard a smile in his voice. "I'm just calling to tell you Timmy and I won't be at the main house today. When you come to visit.... You are coming to visit, aren't you?"

"Uh, yes. After lunch."

"Good. Enter the same way you always do, but about a third of the way down the driveway, you'll see a narrow turnoff on the left. Take that turnoff. You'll find us at the end of the lane."

Suzanna pushed her hand through her long mussed hair, innumerable questions tumbling through her mind.

"I can't really talk now," Logan said. "I'm running late as it is. See you then. Oh, and don't forget your bathing suit."

For a long bemused moment Suzanna sat there staring at the humming receiver. She tried to think mean thoughts: Logan was a snob who didn't feel she was good enough to raise a Bradford; he was arrogant and suspicious, believing she coveted Bradford money....

But hard as she tried, mean thoughts did her no good whatsoever. She flopped back on her pillow, arms flung over her head, and surrendered to the fact that on this brilliantly sunny morning the only thing on her mind was getting back to Mattashaum.

It was almost one o'clock when she came to the turnoff Logan had described. Funny how she'd never noticed it before, how senses could become so emotionally overloaded that something as blatant as another roadway could be missed.

Unpaved and narrow, it cut through the woods for about half a mile before the trees thinned and marshy fields took their place. Soon Suzanna found she was skirting the bank of a broad rippled pond. She slowed her vehicle, trying to get her bearings. Was this Twelve Acre Pond? She could see the ocean glittering to the south, and to the west, on the other side of the pond, the roof of the main house rising through the trees.

"Well, I'll be!" she whispered, a smile lifting her expression.

She hurried up the lane, eager to find out if her guess was right. Sure enough, a cottage came into view, the same cottage she had noticed yesterday from the creek.

Considering the classic architecture of the main house, Suzanna was a little surprised that Logan had chosen to build something so contemporary. She was even more surprised that it looked so comfortable and inviting. Its broad redwood decks beckoning with wind chimes, potted geraniums and several deeply cushioned chairs. She gazed through her dusty windshield, biting her lip—and readjusting her impression of Logan Bradford once again.

A small patch of yard had been mown out of the scrub grass in front, with a path running down the bank through the thicker vegetation toward the pond. Logan was down there with Timmy, sitting in an old wooden rowboat pulled up on the shore. When he heard her van door slam, he got to his feet and waved.

"Down here!" he called. He was wearing loose-fitting tan shorts—and not much else. Even from a distance, the sight of his powerful half-clothed body made breathing difficult. His muscles were too beautifully defined, his skin too perfectly bronzed.

She looked away and forced herself to think about Cecily. Heavenly day, how could she be thinking such lustful thoughts about another woman's fiancé? It was practically adulterous.

But thinking of Cecily didn't do her much good. When Suzanna reached the rowboat and Logan smiled hello, her heart thumped almost painfully.

"Auntie Sue!" Timmy cried.

Thank heaven for little boys and timely diversions, she thought.

"Lookit, me and Unka Logan is having dinner in a boat."

So, he was Uncle Logan already, was he?

But Timmy was giggling so gleefully, today's reaction to her arrival so markedly different from yesterday's, that Suzanna was unable to feel resentful.

"Dinner in a boat? How special. Whatcha havin'?"

"Baloney and plums."

Suzanna's eyes rounded. Timmy didn't usually care for plums.

"Can I help you aboard?" Logan stood, his lofty height making her feel delicate and feminine in comparison.

"Thank you." She handed him her carryall, even though she could have placed it in the boat herself. And when he offered her his hand, she took it, although sliding over the side would've been easier without help. A heightened sense of courtesy seemed to have sprung up between them overnight. At least she thought it was courtesy.

Still tingling from Logan's touch, she took a seat beside her nephew in the stern.

"Would you like a sandwich?" Logan offered, straddling the middle bench and bracing his elbows on the gunwale behind him, drawing attention to the ridges of his broad muscled chest. Suzanna decided he had the most remarkable pectorals she had ever seen.

She realized he was watching her and gulped. "Um, no thanks. I've already eaten." She hoped he thought her heightened color was the result of trekking down the hill in the hot sun.

"Well, let me just straighten house here...." Logan reached for a canvas bag and gathered up wax paper, plastic cups, a large insulated jug. "Would you like to join us for a row?"

Suzanna laughed nervously. "Is this thing safe?"

"Relatively. But then the pond's not too deep. Biggest danger is getting stuck in the muck out there at low tide." He looked over his shoulder at her, at her loose flowing hair, her yellow T-shirt, at her white shorts and long legs.

Suzanna's breath stalled under his perusal. "Is this okay?" She looked down at her outfit, her hair cascading forward. "I'm wearing a bathing suit underneath if—"

"That's fine." His mouth twitched with a suppressed smile. "I was just wondering if you'd put on sunscreen."

"Oh. No, not yet." She grimaced. "I didn't even bring any."

"Here." He tossed her a tube. "Timmy and I are already basted. Help yourself."

"Thank you." While she applied the cream, Logan gave a whistle and Buddy came romping through the reeds.

"Come on, boy," he urged, and the pup leapt eagerly into the boat. Suzanna peeked up from her ministrations, amazed by how quickly Logan had won the dog's allegiance. She knew Logan had a masterful personality, but all that tail-wagging indicated something more.

After strapping Timmy into a life jacket, Logan vaulted out of the boat and pushed it into the water. Before Suzanna could even offer to help, he was back in and sitting opposite her, his lean brown arms plying the heavy wooden oars. With long graceful strokes, he soon had them gliding out across the sky-colored pond. Beside her, Timmy sat bolt upright with anticipation.

Suzanna cast a curious glance from him to Logan. "I guess last night went smoothly?" She hoped the question was oblique enough to get by Timmy, but immediately he perked.

"Auntie Sue, me and Unka Logan—"

"Yes, he was fine," Logan interrupted. "Slept like a log."

Suzanna ignored him. "What were you saying, Tim?"

"Me...me'n Unka Logan slep' over dere." Excitement animated Timmy's whole body. He stood up and pointed to the cottage on the bank.

"That right?" she said, pulling him back down onto the seat. But her eyes were fixed on Logan. "You didn't sleep in Grandpa's house last night?"

"No, I slep' in the underneath bed and Unka Logan slep' on top."

"Bunk beds," Logan explained, eyes narrowed on the horizon as if something of the utmost interest were happening out there. "Don't read anything into it, Suzanna. I merely wanted to be out here early this morning. I had some...things to do."

Of course he did. Just as switching houses had nothing to do with Collin or the anxiety he caused Timmy, or with Suzanna's plea for Logan to remember who was guardian.

Chewing on a small pleased smile, she asked, "And what about Brunhilda?"

Logan tried his utmost to look uninterested. "Oh, she...she was offered a post she couldn't refuse. Brussels."

"Ah." Again Suzanna struggled to conceal a smile. She didn't want to feel grateful, but Logan had made some pretty serious concessions regarding Timmy's care.

Timmy turned to her, almost breathless with excitement. "I...I...I..."

She laughed. "Yes, love?"

"I went to work with Unka Logan this morning!"

Again her eyes shot to Logan's, this time thoroughly surprised.

Timmy continued excitedly, "I saw how dey make..." He paused.

"Windmills," Logan supplied.

"Windmills," the child repeated. "And if... if you got a windmill, you don't got to pay the 'lectric."

Suzanna's brow furrowed. "Oh, I see. The windmill makes electricity for you free, is that it?"

"Yup!" Timmy's tiny bottom wriggled in satisfaction on the hard bench. "And Unka Logan says everybody should have 'em and then...and then..." Obviously having forgotten whatever Logan had said, he slid to the side of the boat and trailed his fingers in the water.

Suzanna wanted to resent Logan for how quickly he'd become a hero to her nephew, but seeing Timmy so genuinely happy canceled out whatever she wanted to feel. In addition, she was too filled with gratitude to feel anything negative.

"Thanks, Logan."

He pulled the oars out of the water and let the boat drift. "For what?"

"Harris used to take Timmy into the studio sometimes. He got such a kick out of going to work with his dad."

"Oh." Logan's voice fell along with his expression.

Suzanna was sorry she'd introduced Harris into the conversation. Obviously he was still a painful subject with his brother.

Just then, however, Timmy let out an astonished shout. "A big fish. Look!"

Suzanna caught sight of a dark blur as it swam away. "That did look pretty big."

"Nice dinner size," Logan commented. "What do you think, Tim. Shall we do a little fishing for our dinner?"

"You didn't bring any poles," Suzanna said.

"No, but I do have a seine."

Curiously Suzanna watched him tear off a bit of what was left of Timmy's sandwich, place it in the net and carefully lower it into the water. Within minutes a fish came calling.

"I don't believe this!" Suzanna exclaimed, impressed by Logan's resourcefulness.

"Scoop some water into that bucket," he instructed, and when she had, he lowered the flapping fish inside. "I'd say that's about a two pounder. Not bad. Shall we try for another?"

When she shrugged uncertainly, he added, "You will be staying for dinner, won't you?"

She was reluctant to say yes because she did want to stay, and the reason, she realized, wasn't just Timmy anymore.

"Of course you're staying," Logan answered for her. "Tim's been planning on it all day."

His words put things back into perspective. Timmy. He was the reason she was here. The only reason.

Logan snared one more fish and then suggested they harvest a few quahogs. "What are you in the mood for? Chowder? Clams casino?"

Suzanna's mouth began to water. What a luxury to have fresh seafood right at one's door. "Clams casino would be great. Oh, what the heck. I'll throw together a chowder, too."

"Uh-uh. I don't care if you are in the catering business. Chowder is *my* specialty."

Suzanna reached into her carryall for a brush and quickly arranged her hair in a French braid while Logan rowed them toward a spit of land in the middle of the pond. He called it Elephant Rock Island and said he'd spent half his adolescence camping out there. A lone tree grew at one end as if to balance the huge boulder at the other. After pulling the boat up to the shore, they all climbed out.

"Tim, leave your sneakers on. You, too, Suzanna. The pond is littered with broken shells. I have a washer and dryer up at the house. You can clean them during dinner."

Suzanna couldn't help but enjoy Logan's thoughtfulness. Granted, his consideration was meant for Timmy and he'd included her only to be polite, but it still felt good to be watched over.

She removed Timmy's shirt, then shrugged off her own clothing and tucked it into her bag. She didn't feel self-conscious until she sensed Logan's eyes on her.

She was wearing a one-piece swimsuit, cut low in the back and high at the thigh, and while the front wasn't inordinately daring, it did reveal a bit of cleavage. Gulping, she glanced up to find him calf deep in water, leaning on a rake, a look of pure male appreciation glinting in his eyes.

Quickly he got to work, pretending he hadn't been watching. She splashed into the water to join him, deciding there was no way she could ask him to apply sunscreen to her back now.

"What do I do?" she asked. "I'm used to getting my shellfish off a truck."

"Spoiled city kid." He shook his head disparagingly, but his eyes still sparkled. "Just dig around until you strike something hard. Might be a rock—" he swished his hand through the water to wash away the mud "—or it might not." In his outstretched palm lay a three-inch wide quahog, the hard-shelled clam native to the region. "This is too big for clams casino. What we're after are little necks," he explained, using the local term for a smaller, more tender size. "I'll hang on to this one, though. We can grind it for our chowder. Hey, Tim, stay close by, okay?"

"Okeydokey," the child somehow answered amid all his splashing, which appeared to be an imitation of the stroke his puppy was doing.

Logan floated a plastic bucket between himself and Suzanna and handed her a small garden rake. But just as she was leaning over ready to dig, he gripped her arm. "Wait. Hold it."

"What now?"

He sloshed over to the boat. When he returned, the tube of sunscreen was in his hand. "Turn around."

A small current of tension buzzed through her. "I'm okay, really."

"What you are is pale as a mushroom. What you're going to be is burnt toast." Without waiting for her approval, he turned her around and slathered on a palmful of cream, warm from the sun.

Suzanna stood very still, trying to concentrate on the wind-stunted oak on the tiny island. Stood very still, while his strong callused hand stroked down the middle of her back and up to one shoulder. Tried to think of painful sun blisters, as wave upon wave of pleasurable sensation shivered through her.

"That should do it." He gave her back a friendly slap.

She opened her eyes, unaware of having closed them. Good glory, what was happening to her! "Th-thank you." Quickly she dived into her digging.

"Hey, Tim, want to give it a try?" Logan called.

Suzanna glanced up, surprised. Timmy was too young to help, she thought, watching Logan lean over the child to show him how to drag the small rake.

Within minutes, though, when Timmy held out his hand, beaming, she changed her mind. There was so much for him to learn here—about the balance of nature, about self-sufficiency. About peace of mind.

Within a half hour, they'd gathered more than enough shellfish for their meal. Logan placed the bucket in the boat and then walked Suzanna and Timmy onto the tiny island, pointing out his favorite spot to build a fire and where he'd chiseled his initials into the rock. They sat for a long while, talking and sipping cool lemonade poured from the jug.

Suzanna was enthralled by his stories about Mattashaum, about the Indian artifacts he'd found in the woods and the wide variety of plants and animal life within its boundaries. As she listened, happiness settled into a place deep inside her. And peace. She felt a wealth of peace here— which didn't make sense since she was keeping company with a man diametrically opposed to everything she was striving for. Yet here on this tiny island, with nothing more jarring than the occasional squawk of a gull, family rancor and courtroom battles seemed part of another life.

"LET ME HANDLE one of the oars," Suzanna offered when they returned to the boat. "I've never rowed before, but it doesn't look too hard."

"I won't refuse the help." Logan made room for her on his bench.

After a few awkward pulls she was puffing. "This is like poling through hot tar."

Logan threw back his head and laughed. She smiled, no longer aware of what she'd said but only of how much she liked the small fan of lines at the corners of his eyes.

Despite the heaviness of the oar, she soon got the hang of what she was doing, and before long she and Logan had synchronized their movements into a smooth rhythm. She felt wonderful—healthy, alive, happy—even with silt squishing grittily in her sneakers.

"What a lovely day!" She sighed dreamily.

Logan smiled up at the deep blue sky. "Mmm. I love September. Water's had the whole summer to warm. The haze is gone. Unfortunately fall will be upon us soon."

"Which makes these days even more precious, don't you think? You pay attention to them more, knowing they're about to end."

Although Logan kept rowing, his stroke was slightly off rhythm, and she noticed his smile had faded. "Yes," was all he said.

He missed his brother, Suzanna thought. She didn't know how she'd arrived at that idea, but she was sure he was thinking about Harris.

"So, tell me about last night. How did you two guys end up sleeping at the cottage?"

Her ploy worked. Logan's frown dissolved as he launched into an explanation.

Just as she'd predicted, Timmy had only slept for three hours and then awakened. And, no, he hadn't been too upset by her not being there—well, just a little, Logan admitted. Mrs. Travis had fed them supper in the kitchen, and then they'd packed their bags and left.

"In the end it turned into a pretty good time. Like a camp-out."

"And are you sleeping there again tonight?"

"Er...yes."

Suzanna leaned into her rowing with a smile, feeling the world had finally begun to right itself.

As they rowed, their arms sometimes brushed, and at first, Suzanna was startled by the electrifying contact and tried to distance herself. Logan's skin was hot, his muscles as hard as they looked. But the longer they bumped and brushed, the more she enjoyed the shivers that raced through her. Finally she caught herself actually moving closer so that their arms *would* brush.

When the bow finally scraped up on the shore below Logan's cottage, she felt reluctant to move. Sitting beside her, Logan lifted his oar out of the water and leaned forward to slide it out of the lock. When he did, his thigh pressed hers, and flame spread through her. She didn't dare look at him, yet didn't move away. And neither did he. It was as if they were testing something they weren't quite sure of yet. The flame grew hotter, until finally Suzanna was sure heat must be pulsing off her skin in visible waves.

She stared at the muddy deck of the boat, alarmed that she hadn't been able to shake off this attraction, not even with reminders that he was engaged. From the deck, her eyes traveled to his sneaker, and from his sneaker up his ankle to a lower leg that was roughened by a thin covering of dark hair. What a beautiful leg, she thought in dismay. Even his knee was perfect.

She lifted her eyes quickly and swallowed, finding him studying her, too. By now her hair was probably a fright, loose ends branching out from her French braid like the snakes of a Medusa head. Still, when his admiring eyes met hers, when she noticed the sensuous curve of his mouth, her heart took an ecstatic leap.

"Auntie Sue?"

Suzanna sucked in a breath so deep she realized she mustn't have been breathing for a while. "Yes, love."

But the child had nothing to ask her. He only gazed at her and then at Logan—and smiled.

They both moved at once, jumping into self-conscious activity. They secured the boat, unloaded their catch, packed clothing and headed up the path, all the while talking to Timmy, their safe common bond.

This couldn't be happening, Suzanna thought frantically. Not with Logan Bradford. It was one thing to find him a physically attractive specimen of the male population, but quite another to start playing eye games and...and feeling things for that gorgeous specimen. In addition to all the obvious reasons, he was engaged. Why couldn't she get that fact to register?

They took turns showering, Suzanna first, then Timmy and Logan together. Clothing got put in the washer, soft music on the stereo, and while Timmy built castles with his wooden blocks on the dining-room rug, Suzanna and Logan prepared dinner in the adjoining kitchen.

"That was a lot easier than I thought it would be," Logan commented, sitting down to eat.

Suzanna flipped open her napkin. "You're very efficient in the kitchen. You must've had practice."

"Some."

"I'd say a lot." She paused to make up Timmy's plate. "You live here, don't you?"

"Whatever gave you that idea?" He seemed inordinately preoccupied with buttering his bread.

"The huge number of books, the magazines and stray sweaters. This place is filled with you, Logan."

"I stay here occasionally, I told you that. Mmm, this fish is really good."

Suzanna tasted a forkful of the succulent fish and agreed. He obviously didn't want anyone prying into his personal life, and they'd been getting along too well for her to push the issue.

"By the way, I love this place." She smiled softly.

The dining room, like the living room and kitchen, was glass-walled and faced southwest. From where they sat, they had a panoramic view of the pond, meadows and dunes, and the ocean beyond. The westering sun slanted low over it all, causing colors to practically throb.

"Thank you. I like it, too. By the way, I designed it." As if that weren't enough to impress her, he went on to talk about the construction company that had built it, a company he had formed and was still expanding.

As she listened, Suzanna leaned on her hand, staring at his impossibly handsome face. What day was this? she wondered. When had they stopped being enemies? Time seemed to have warped so that two days felt like two months. And this dinner... this dinner felt like heaven.

Smiling down on Timmy, Logan wiped his mouth and placed the napkin alongside his plate. The boy had been growing noticeably sleepy through the meal. Now his head lay on the table and he was humming in a languid monotone. Logan's eyes burned with a love that seemed too deep after so short a time. But of course, Timmy was family, and that alone entitled him to Logan's protection and affection.

Without warning, Suzanna felt a knife-twist of envy toward the woman who'd soon be Mrs. Logan Bradford. How glorious to be the object of such fierce loyalty.

"Have you and Cecily set a date for your wedding?" she asked, tracing a pattern on the tabletop with her thumbnail.

Logan seemed surprised by the question. "Uh, no." Then he scowled. "We haven't been engaged all that long."

"Will you be living here after you get married?"

Logan pushed a hand through his hair. "Yes. No. I have no idea." They both fell quiet, both carving patterns in the tablecloth now. "What about you?" His scowl deepened until he looked positively thunderous. "Are you seeing anyone seriously?"

And why would he be asking her that? She shook her head, damp hair tossing the fragrance of Logan's shampoo about her like an intoxicating spell. "These past few years I haven't had much time to date, let alone carry on a serious relationship."

Strangely his scowl eased. But the tension between them didn't. If anything, it grew, filling the room until she almost couldn't breathe.

She pushed herself up from the table. "I...I really should be going. Let me help clear the table and—"

Timmy suddenly lifted his tired head. "Where you going?"

"It's time for me to leave now, Tim. I'll see you again tomorrow."

"No!" His eyes took on a glassiness that had nothing to do with sleep. Suddenly he launched himself from his chair and threw his arms around her legs. "No. You stay."

"Timmy! I'll be back."

But he burst into tears. "Stay. You stay." His sobs were heartbreaking.

Suzanna stroked his hair, her mind awash. "Honey, I'll be here bright and early. You'll hardly know I was gone."

"No! I'll be good. I won't let Buddy chew the candy anymore. I promise I'll be good." He clung to her legs, his tears soaking into her clothing.

"Oh, dear Lord!" Suzanna whispered, her own teary eyes lifting to Logan's. She'd imagined all sorts of dreadful repercussions from Timmy's being moved from her care, but this she hadn't anticipated. She got down on her knees and held his racking body close.

"Honey, you did nothing wrong. I'm not leaving because Buddy chewed the shower favors. You're a good boy. The best."

She looked up at the man standing silhouetted against the pale evening sky. "Oh, Logan, we've got a problem."

His sigh was weary. "I know."

"May I take him home, just for tonight?"

He turned to stare out the window. "You could stay here. I think that would be a better alternative."

Timmy's sobs subsided a bit, his attention sharpening.

"Stay here? Me?"

"Yes. The house has three bedrooms."

"But..."

"No buts. Nights are his worst times. If you have to leave in the morning to see to your job, I'm sure he'll be fine. But the nights... Stay, Suzanna." His voice was low and tired.

She pried Timmy's arms from around her neck and set him a little distance away. "So, what do you say, kiddo? Think I ought to sleep over?"

With his mouth still turned downward and trembling, Timmy nodded. She kissed his cheek and hugged him again before getting to her feet.

"Okay, Mr. Bradford. Looks like you've got another guest."

CHAPTER EIGHT

LOGAN SLID the patio door shut behind him and walked across the redwood deck. A quarter moon was hanging like a silver charm over the darkly glittering ocean, while somewhere toward the point a robin trilled a joyous song. Objectively he could see it was a beautiful evening, but he felt only misery. He lowered himself, like an old man, he thought, onto the top step and dropped his head into his hands.

When he'd heard Timmy's sobs, seen the terror in his eyes, he'd thought he might come unglued. What sort of unholy business had he become a party to? And how much worse was it going to get before it got better?

Logan was doing everything he could to make Timmy feel secure and provided for, but apparently his efforts weren't enough. Apparently Suzanna provided something that all the wealth on earth couldn't buy. He pressed the heels of his hands against his eyes and felt a sense of failure that cut right to his core.

Behind him the patio door sighed open. He dropped his hands but didn't turn around lest the light from the house reveal the worry in his face.

"Is he asleep?" From the corner of his eye, he watched Suzanna's bare toes curl over the edge of the step beside him.

Timmy hadn't fully believed she was staying over until she'd put her bag on the upper bunk in his room and changed into nightclothes, which since she hadn't brought any, had been improvised from Logan's wardrobe: a T-shirt that reached to her knees and a robe of navy cotton he rarely wore.

"Yes," she answered. "He drifted off almost as soon as his head hit the pillow."

Logan glanced up. "Really?"

She sat beside him, and the robe slid open, revealing long silky legs. Despite his misery, he thought she looked adorable in his outsize clothing, hair tumbling free and her complexion glowing with new vibrancy from the sun.

"Sure. He was really exhausted. He had quite a day."

Logan set his grim gaze on the crescent moon. "I'm sorry," he mumbled. Immediately he wished he'd had more control. How foolish to admit he was wrong—to Suzanna, of all people. She was going to take the admission and ride him into the ground with it.

The night fell silent between them.

"You don't have to apologize. It was a good day. Healthful, active, happy."

Logan was too surprised by her reaction to speak for a moment. Maybe he could discuss his concerns with her, after all. "But that spell of crying, that sudden fear and sadness—where did it come from, Suzanna? He was doing so well."

She turned to look at him more directly. He felt her scrutiny like a hot searchlight. "You're really worried, aren't you?"

"Of course I'm worried. Aren't you?"

"Believe it or not, I've been through worse with him."

Logan couldn't imagine worse. "It hasn't been easy, has it?"

Her sigh spoke volumes.

On impulse, Logan reached over and placed a sympathetic hand on her back. "You have to believe me when I say I really thought moving him here was in his best interests."

"Crazy as it sounds, I do believe you. That's why I'm not as angry as I should be. And I should be furious. I believe you're a more honorable man than I originally thought. You assumed you were doing the right thing, even though it wasn't, and now that you've seen the result, I believe you'll choose to do the honorable thing again and ... and correct the harm you've done."

Logan narrowed his eyes. "And how exactly would I do that?"

"By dropping this guardianship contest and letting Timmy go home with me where he belongs."

"You don't quit, do you?"

"No."

He rose abruptly. "Well, neither do I." He paced to the end of the deck where he stood scowling across the pond. In the far distance, a dim light glowed from the main house.

"Suzanna, look, I don't want to argue." He thrust his hand through his hair. He so wanted her to understand him, an attitude he found disturbing. He'd never been concerned about explaining himself in the past.

"I thought Timmy's coming here was right for a lot of reasons. I still do." He couldn't bear to see his nephew return to the city, to that tiny fenced yard, to the threat of crime and living on the financial edge. But how could he tell Suzanna these things without insulting her?

He heard her get up. He turned and watched her slowly advance, idly tapping a wind chime on the way. With her long shapely legs, graceful arms and swanlike neck, she was elegance itself, and suddenly he realized he didn't much like the idea of her returning to the city, either.

"So?" she said, leaning against the rail a short distance away from him. "What are those reasons?"

With a shake of his head, he tried to separate himself from his growing fascination with her. "Aside from everything that was said in court? Well, for one thing I thought it would be good for Collin to have his grandson here."

She choked out a deprecating laugh.

"I'm serious. He's aged noticeably since Harris's death, and I thought—"

"Timmy would rejuvenate him?"

"Yes."

"Give me a break."

Logan gripped her arm and turned her to face him. "I know you don't think much of my father because of the way he treated Harris...." He paused, unsure he wanted to get into private family histories with Suzanna. But then, if she was going to understand him and the love he bore his father, she had to understand Collin, as well.

"But what you don't know about that old man is that he was so distraught by Harris's leaving he had a heart attack. He nearly died, Suzanna."

Logan watched the information sink in and register. Suzanna's beautiful face looked aggrieved.

"I didn't know. Good Lord, Harris didn't know."

"I chose not to tell him. I...." Logan shook off the reason.

"No wonder you were so angry with your brother." Her eyes were wide, staring at him as if for the first time. "But surely you don't blame poor Harris for the heart attack. Your father strikes me as a very high-strung person, and heavens, I've even seen him smoking."

Logan sighed. Yes, Collin smoked, despite his doctor's orders. Collin did whatever the hell Collin pleased—as if he were above the laws that governed other people.

"No, I don't blame Harris for Collin's poor health, but he didn't help matters any, either. He was stubborn and argumentative.... But I'm straying from my purpose. What I wanted to say was that my father is a more complicated person than you think. A more *feeling* person. He may have his faults, but who doesn't? And as far as I can see he has more reason for having them than most people."

"Like?"

"For starters, how does the idea of his father committing suicide grab you?"

Suzanna went absolutely still. "His father...what?"

"Got into his Duesenberg one day, jacked it up to ninety on a winding back road and aimed it at a tree. Of course, no one could prove it was suicide but..."

"Was it the depression? Did he lose a lot in the stock-market crash?"

Logan shook his head. "He was too shrewd. Good times, bad times, we Bradfords have always survived. No, from what I've been able to gather, my grandfather's problem was he was diagnosed with a terminal illness at the age of forty-two. He was a proud man and couldn't abide the thought of becoming an invalid and a burden to his family."

"But suicide? How old was Collin?"

"Eleven."

She winced. "That's awful."

"Damn right it's awful. What's also awful is having your wife leave you for another man."

Suzanna squared her shoulders, her antagonism returning. "The way I heard it, Collin drove your mother away. She couldn't take his coldness anymore."

Logan paced a few steps, paced back, feeling emotions too complex to sort. "Harry never would allow Collin any leeway when it came to my mother." He sighed, a sound that seemed to come from his toes. "Let's go inside. I could use a drink."

They returned to the living room where Logan poured them each a cognac and invited her to sit on the sofa beside him.

"Harry was only two when my mother left, far too young to understand why."

"Oh, and you did?"

At an onslaught of memories, Logan felt a vise tighten around his heart—memories of empty days when he and Harry were ignored, of dark nights thick with whispered arguments. "No," he answered sadly. "I didn't understand. Not fully. I still don't. Other people's lives are unfathomable, Suzanna. So many reasons behind reasons. That's why I resist assigning blame to any one side."

He watched her frown, her long elegant hands nervously smoothing the fabric of his robe over her thighs. "Are you trying to say that Collin's father's death and his wife's leaving are somehow related?"

Logan nodded thoughtfully. "He's never really talked about his father's death—he doesn't talk about anything personal—but I do believe he was deeply disturbed by it, and molded by it. At eleven years of age, he had to've viewed it as a desertion and, as such, a failure of love. He certainly waited long enough before he married. Didn't have me until he was forty."

"Hmm. Harris said he married only to have children. Heirs," she amended.

"That's possible, though I really think Collin loved my mother. No, I *know* he did. He was devastated when she left, just as he was when Harris left. But he couldn't express his feelings. Still can't. And the reasons for that—" Logan raised his hands, palms up "—are legion. You could say he came from a long line of undemonstrative tight-lipped Yankees. Could say it was his brooding Calvinist roots. Could be he was afraid to put his heart on the line again and love anyone the way he'd loved his father. Or maybe, maybe it's as simple as he's seventy-two years old, Suzanna. Men of his generation just weren't raised expressing feelings. Emotions belonged to women, and expressing them revealed vulnerability."

Logan tipped back the remainder of his cognac and sank more comfortably into the cushions. His muscles felt pleasantly stretched from the exertion of the day, his skin tight and warm from the sun. But mostly he was feeling something he hadn't ever felt before—a closeness, an intimacy.

He gazed at Suzanna's beautifully sculpted face, softly lit by the lamp behind her, gazed into her smoky green eyes, and wondered why? Why her? What was it about Suzanna Keating that broke down his normal reserve and made him want to talk? Talk? Good Lord, he wanted to lay out his life and let her dance all over it.

"So, what you're saying is your grandfather's suicide set a pattern that recurred often enough in Collin's life for him to come to the conclusion that nobody can be trusted?"

"That love can't be trusted," Logan clarified. "It certainly didn't have the power to hold the people *he* loved in place."

"Ah!" Suzanna's eyes glittered. "So that explains his attempts to control people with money."

"Exactly." Logan draped his arm over the back of the sofa and gave her a long careful look. Suzanna wasn't just beautiful; she was sharp, and talking with her was becoming an addiction.

"I have one question. *Did* your mother have an affair?"

Logan refilled his glass and stared for a long while at the amber liquid before taking a sip. "Yes. She never denied it."

"Oh." Suzanna settled back, looking disappointed.

Logan contemplated telling her she'd probably been right about Collin's cold personality driving his mother away. He remembered the night he tiptoed from his room to listen in at his parents' door and heard her pleading for forgiveness. Until that night he'd sided with his father, feeling righteous about Collin's anger. But that night he'd seen the situation in a new light. He'd become confused, unsure and later, when his mother was gone and the loneliness set in, outraged.

Collin could have forgiven her, could have tried to make a new start. People did it all the time. But once wounded by someone, Collin never trusted that person again. And though he'd suffered without end as a result of his own stubbornness, and though his wife didn't remarry for several years, giving him ample time to change his mind, he never did. He became intractable, cruelly and unnecessarily intractable. As he'd been with Harris.

"I don't know." Suzanna shook her head in doubt.

"Don't know what?"

"If I believe Collin's really the sweet sensitive guy you want me to think he is. That choice he forced Harris to make. It still strikes me as terribly cruel."

"I didn't say sweet and sensitive, Suzanna. I said complex. He has reasons for doing and saying the things he does, murky multifaceted reasons he isn't even aware of himself, but basically I believe they're all rooted in his love for his family and his need to be loved and to feel assured we aren't going to desert him."

Suzanna reached over and placed her hand lightly on his forearm, her long fingers patting sympathetically.

Logan sighed, shook his head. "I could be wrong of course. It isn't easy to understand another person's life. It's even harder to judge that life, and so I don't try. The best I hope to be is tolerant, especially of elderly people. They've lived through so many experiences and are carrying so much baggage how *can* I judge them?"

The pressure of Suzanna's hand increased and suddenly became the focus of his entire existence. He turned his head and let his gaze pour over her lovely face. Soon the conversation was forgotten, everything dissolved except the overwhelming desire to kiss her.

WITH A START, Suzanna realized her hand was resting on Logan's arm. She jerked it back to her lap and fixed her gaze on the dark sliding shadows outside the cottage.

She still had her doubts about Collin and the excuses Logan supplied for his behavior. It was much easier to side with Harris's opinion—that Collin was simply a devious and manipulative tyrant who enjoyed controlling people.

What she had absolutely no doubt about, however, was that Logan was the most tolerant man she'd ever met, a man she could quite easily fall in love with. And if she wasn't very careful, that was exactly what was going to happen.

She felt his gaze on her and with breathless caution turned her head. His eyes were heavy-lidded and warm, his mouth relaxed, his long-limbed body indolent, everything about him beckoning her with a sleepy sensuality that sent heat curling right down to her toes.

As if watching a film over which she had no control, she saw Logan lean in, saw his head tilt, felt his hand cradle the back of her head, felt his warm lips touch hers—and the heat curling through her fanned into fire. Her eyes drifted closed of their own volition, and the soft pressure of his mouth increased.

He kissed the way he did everything—wonderfully. When he finally backed away, Suzanna was a wreck. Her heartbeat was a blur and her mind was a fevered blank.

"Well," he whispered, a slow smile lifting one corner of his mouth. "Now we know."

Suzanna could barely speak. "Know w-what?"

"About the fascination we've felt for each other these past two years." His low intimate voice sent shivers cascading over her skin.

"T-two...?"

"Mmm. Since that party you catered out on the point."

Her cheeks burned. "You realized that was me?"

His fathomless gray eyes sparkled, slowly taking in her thick curling hair, then moving over her hot face, feature by feature, as if he was enjoying a work of art. "Oh, yes. Not at first of course. Not until I asked Barbara about you."

"Barbara?"

"The woman who had the party. Did you know who I was?"

"No. Not until shortly before you left."

"We must've found out at about the same time. Once I realized who I'd been eyeing all night, I felt it was better to leave." Logan touched a finger to her cheek, running it down to her lips, tracing their contour and stopping at the small beauty mark. "I must say, Barbara saved me from making a colossal fool of myself just in the nick of time."

Suzanna blinked, lost for a moment, and then it came flooding back, the humiliation she'd felt upon discovering his identity. How ridiculous she would have felt if they had gone the extra step and spoken—she, Claudia's sister, he, Harris's brother.

And in the next instant she remembered his leaving that party two years ago—with Cecily.

Cecily!

Suzanna pulled in a breath and backed away from Logan carefully. "It's really a pity Barbara isn't here now, Mr. Bradford."

She watched him frown.

"Seems you just made colossal fools of us both."

Before he could see the tears in her eyes, she bolted from the sofa and ran to her room.

LOGAN STARED at the closed bedroom door for several long minutes, unable to believe he'd allowed himself to forget about Cecily. He couldn't imagine what Suzanna thought of him now. Or maybe he could, and that was the problem.

He took a step toward the bedroom, every instinct wanting to explain that he wasn't really engaged, that he hadn't just compromised a serious relationship. But if he did, Suzanna would know that he'd lied before the judge and, worse, that the lie had helped him take Timmy away from her. By exonerating himself in one area, he'd be damning himself in another.

He clutched the back of his neck and muttered a few choice epithets.

Ah, well, served him right, he thought. Even if he wasn't trapped within this idiotic ruse, he still shouldn't have allowed himself to forget who Suzanna was. As attracted as he was to her, far too many issues stood between them for a relationship to develop. No, the best thing to do was continue the charade.

Of course, he'd have to think of something to tell her in the morning, something to explain that kiss....

For an unguarded moment, a smile crept over Logan's face. What a kiss it had been! An intoxicating blend of innocence and heat, discovery and promises....

But they were promises that could never be kept. He had to remember that. His smile cooled. He wasn't looking forward to the morning. Not looking forward to it at all.

THE NEXT MORNING Suzanna awoke to the aroma of freshly perked coffee. She opened her eyes to find a ceiling just a couple of feet above her. With a start, she remembered where she was—the upper bunk of a bed in Logan's house. She rolled onto her hip and, gripping the bed rail, peeked over the side to see if Timmy was still asleep below.

"Yih!" she yelped, coming nose to nose with Logan, instead.

"Sorry. Didn't mean to startle you." He was dressed in loose pajama bottoms that rode low on his waist, drawing attention to the broad expanse of muscular chest above it. He was holding up a mug to her.

"For me? Thank you." She sat up, ducking a little to avoid hitting her head on the ceiling, and took a sip of the coffee. It was just as she liked it. "Is Timmy up yet?"

"Yes, he's in the kitchen having breakfast. We thought we'd let you sleep in a bit."

"How is he?"

"Cheerful. Rested. The transformation's amazing."

Suzanna took another sip, aware that he was watching her. Aware, too, that they were both thinking about the previous night and the intimacy that had blossomed between them. Logan might have blundered, but then so had she. She'd done nothing to stop him from kissing her, and when he had, she'd thoroughly enjoyed the experience. Now her head ached from trying to come up with something she could say to salvage her pride.

Abruptly she handed back the mug. "I'm not used to breakfast in bed. Let me get up and about." She scrambled down, trying to stop Logan's T-shirt from riding up around her thighs. As soon as she landed she wrapped herself in his robe.

"Suzanna, wait." Logan gripped her arm when she would have hurried past him. His gentle tug brought her into contact with his warm, hair-coarsened chest, an electrifying contact that turned her knees to rubber. She knew she should back away, but mesmerized by the pleasurable sensations washing through her, she lingered awhile, as did he. Only slowly did they draw apart.

"What?" she asked, lowering her gaze.

"About last night..."

She grimaced. "I know, I know."

They both sighed, each conveying enough disgust with themselves to invoke sympathy from the other.

"It was a mistake," Logan said.

"Oh, I agree."

"I don't know what happened."

"Curiosity. You said it yourself."

He pounced on the excuse. "Yes, of course. We felt a certain physical attraction...."

"Chemistry. That's all it was."

"Right. And for a moment there..." Logan swallowed.

Suzanna looked everywhere but at him. For a moment there...what? "Emotional exhaustion," she offered. "We were both wiped out after Timmy's tantrum and..."

"And turned to each other for solace."

"Yes, solace." That was it. And curiosity and chemistry. They would extricate themselves from this quagmire yet.

"I trust you agree that the issue can be dropped, then?" Logan fidgeted with the drawstring of his pajama bottoms.

"Absolutely."

"And Cecily needn't hear...?"

"Not from me."

Logan heaved a sigh of relief. "Good. And I assume you and I can continue to cooperate regarding Timmy's care?"

Suzanna picked up her mug and took a sip, finally feeling her feet touch solid ground. "Of course we'll continue to cooperate. For Timmy's well-being, we don't have any choice."

He nodded in a contemplative rhythm. "Good. Good. Then this...problem is behind us?"

"What problem?"

He smiled. "Let's go have breakfast. I have something else to discuss with you."

Suzanna told herself the incident was indeed behind them. Yet, as she followed Logan out of the bedroom, it occurred to her that, in all the babble they'd cluttered the air with, neither of them had actually said they were sorry the kiss had happened.

"AUNTIE SUE! You waked up?" Timmy warbled happily from the kitchen table.

"Yes, I waked up. Good morning, love." Suzanna kissed his velvet cheek. He kissed her in return, his lips cool with milk from his cereal.

Suddenly Suzanna was fighting back a smile. Timmy was wearing green plaid shorts, a blue-and-yellow striped shirt and red socks.

"Did you pick out your clothes today?"

"Yup. All by myself."

Her eyes met Logan's. He shrugged his eyebrows in an expression so comical she laughed. It pleased her inordinately that he'd let Timmy know the satisfaction of making his own choices, but what pleased her even more was the fact that he hadn't criticized or corrected those choices.

"What *I* do," she said out of the side of her mouth, passing Logan on the way to her chair, "is lay out two or three matched outfits and *then* let him choose."

Logan winked. "I'll remember that next time." He set out two more bowls and handed her the cereal box. Sunlight streamed through the tall windows, falling in golden bars across the beautifully defined muscles of his chest. His jaw was darkly shadowed, his hair in need of combing.

Suzanna tried to keep her gaze averted, but his comfortable, rumpled, early-morning looks were just too enticing. "So, what did you want to discuss?" she inquired, her eyes darting from the table to him repeatedly.

"A daily schedule," he answered.

Just then Timmy got off his seat and picked up a bag of toy trucks. "Can I go outside?"

"Sure, pal. But stay right out back where we can see you," Logan answered.

"Okeydokey. Come on, Buddy."

As soon as the screen slid shut, Logan continued, "I think we ought to arrange regular hours to be with Timmy, a schedule that'll allow us to tend to our work and yet be with him, too."

"I thought we were already doing that."

"What I have in mind is alternating shifts so he doesn't have to go along with me to work."

"You mean while you're at the factory, I'd be here with him?"

"Yes, and I'll watch him while you're at work."

"Sounds...efficient." She lowered her eyes, trying to hide her disappointment. The arrangement didn't allow them any overlapping time. Immediately she was angry at herself for feeling disappointed. She was not here to be with Logan.

"What's the matter?" Logan lay down his spoon.

"Nothing."

"What?" he insisted.

She latched onto the best excuse she could think of. "Maybe you can manage working half days, but I can barely make ends meet working..." She didn't finish the sentence. The last thing she needed was to admit to Logan Bradford that she was having financial problems.

She lifted her chin. "What's easier for you? Mornings or afternoons?"

"Mornings. If I start at eight, I can be back here by twelve-thirty. That way you can be back at your place by one, one-thirty. Is that convenient for you?"

"I can make it work."

"Good. I'm not particular about when you return—dinnertime or later in the evening—"

Her eyes snapped wide open. "You want me to come back?"

"Well...yes. Tim slept so peacefully with you here, I took it for granted we'd continue the arrangement."

A pulse throbbed at her temple. "For how long?"

"I don't know. Until he's adjusted."

Suzanna dragged her hands down her face and groaned. Now she *was* worried. She'd been counting on the nights for catching up on her work.

"How's this going to go over with Collin?" she asked.

"That's of no consequence."

She cast a skeptical glance across the table.

"Speaking of my father, I'd like to make visits to him a regular part of Timmy's day. What do you think?"

Suzanna resisted the idea at first, but then, Collin *was* Timmy's grandfather, the only grandparent he had. "How long would these visits be?"

"Short, but enough for Timmy and Collin to get to know one another gradually. I'd arrange the visits around a structured activity, too, a board game or a session currying Timmy's pony."

Suzanna was touched that Logan had consulted her before going ahead with his idea. "I guess it'll be all right. Just...stay with them, okay?"

"Of course."

"I have another question. How's Cecily going to handle my sleeping over?"

Logan sipped his coffee, gaze averted. "What do you mean?"

"Well, will I be..." Uneasiness set in. "Will my presence here upset any, um, sleeping arrangements you two might have come to enjoy, occasional or, um, otherwise?" Her face felt so hot she was sure it was glowing.

Logan's lips twitched in obvious amusement. Suzanna suffered the distinct urge to douse him with her cereal.

"No, Cecily and I will manage."

"Are you sure? I mean, since I've started coming here, you two haven't gone out. I don't think I've even heard you talking on the phone."

She noticed his expression turn pensive. "No, we've talked," he replied, but his tone was distracted. "Honestly, you won't be disturbing us."

"Well, if you're sure...okay, for Timmy's sake I'll stay over. But you owe me, Bradford, big time."

"Repaying you will be my pleasure." The corner of his mouth cocked in a smile that curled her toenails. "Now can we discuss what's really got you worried?"

CHAPTER NINE

SUZANNA REARED BACK. "I don't know what you mean."

"Ever since I brought up the subject of your sleeping over, you've had these two deep furrows between your brows." Logan reached across the table and massaged the spot with the tips of his fingers, a soothing circular motion that soon had her sighing.

It was so unfair, she thought, that someone who was off-limits to her should have such wonderful hands.

"Is it us?" he asked, sitting back. "Are you afraid that what happened last night will be repeated?"

Suzanna shook her head although that possibility was very much on her mind.

"Then it's your work."

She stiffened. When had he learned to read her so well?

"I thought so. Tell me about it."

"What do you want to know?" Suzanna's gaze followed the coffee cup he was raising, and when it met his lips, her own warmed and tingled.

"How it operates. Who does what."

"I can't imagine why—"

"Humor me. I like solving problems."

"I don't have any problems."

"No? Then where'd those dark circles under your eyes come from?"

"Oh." She touched her cheekbone in dismay. "Well, if you really want to hear about it...." Hesitantly she began to fill him in.

Within minutes Logan interrupted her, claiming he'd heard enough. "Seems to me the solution is as plain as day. What you've got to do is take a more managerial role."

"More managerial?" she mocked. "Logan, I'm hardly running General Motors."

"Doesn't matter. Big business, small business, principles are the same."

She shook her head, annoyed by his simplistic advice.

"I mean it. Why do *you* have to have your hand in every aspect of the operation? Why do *you* have to chop celery and scour sinks, as well as play maid and keep the books?"

"My parents always did it that way. Total involvement."

"So? It's obvious that total involvement is wearing you down."

"I love my job," she protested, feeling her throat begin to tighten.

"You do? Tell me, what do you like about it?"

"Well, I love being my own boss, setting my own hours...." Nervously she picked at a loose thread on the bathrobe he'd lent her. She'd never been her own boss, never set her own hours. The business had always run *her*.

"That *is* an advantage to owning your own business. But what do you like about the work?"

Her throat continued to tighten. "It's a good livelihood," she said, scraping back her chair and gathering up the breakfast things. "And I'm very grateful to have it."

Logan rose to help. "You still haven't answered my question."

Suzanna placed the cereal bowls in the sink and closed her eyes. "If you want to know the truth, I don't know what I enjoy. When survival is the reason you work, you don't ask yourself whether you're having a good time or not. You just put one foot in front of the other and get on with it. If I didn't, it wouldn't be long before I'd be out on the street. And if I'm on the street..." Her gaze went to Timmy, playing contentedly on the sunny deck. She sighed and shook her head. "Forget it. I'm probably just too tired to enjoy anything right now."

Having put away the milk, Logan walked toward her, his face lined with concern. "That's what I was getting at. Can't you hire a couple of extra people to do the drudge work?"

She chuckled. "And how do you propose I pay these extra people?"

"By increasing the volume of your business. Concentrate on advertising. Think up new ventures. Be the brains of the operation, not the brawn." He smiled, tipping up her chin so that she had to meet his gaze. "You could do that right here, mornings, while you're spending time with Timmy."

She didn't want to be intrigued by his idea. It was clearly the idea of someone spoiled and rich who had no concept of reality. "You're certifiable, know that?" She didn't want to smile, either, or be so conscious of the heat radiating from his bare chest, or feel so languid under the light stroking of his thumb along her jaw. But she was all those things, and more.

"Think about it, anyway. If anyone can turn that business of yours around, it's you." Genuine admiration filled his voice—and his eyes. For a moment Suzanna felt the gap between them closing, and she wondered, was he leaning in or was it she?

Oh, Lord, he was going to kiss her again. But what really worried her was the fact that there was nothing she wanted more than to be kissed. By him. Only him.

This attraction, despite their attempts to trivialize it, was clearly a force with a mind of its own. Mustering a great deal of willpower, she stepped away and resumed clearing the table. But she was shaken.

"You realize this is a new problem, don't you, one you created by insisting on bringing Timmy here. Before you interfered I was able to be with him all day and still work." Perhaps if she reminded him, and herself, that they were still adversaries, they'd be able to put a damper on this forbidden electricity sizzling between them.

"I'm not too thrilled about cutting back my work hours, either, Suzanna, but Tim is worth the sacrifice. Look at him."

She did. Timmy had abandoned his toys on the deck and was now stalking a fat wild rabbit who'd wandered into the yard to nibble on the dewy grass. The child looked so intense, each tiptoed step taken with such exacting care, that his outstretched arms seesawed like a tightrope walker's.

Suzanna's gaze roamed to the old wooden rowboat pulled up on the shore of the peaceful pond, then across the far dunes to the glittering ocean beyond. Simultaneously she thought of the cramped quarters at her shop where Timmy was forced to entertain himself, often underfoot, and she felt increasingly muddled. Two weeks ago her position had seemed so unquestionably right, but the better she got to know Logan, the faster issues were fading to shades of gray.

"I'll see what I can arrange," she conceded.

After Logan left for work, Suzanna phoned Marie and gave her instructions on what needed doing at the shop that morning. Then she dressed in yesterday's freshly laundered shorts and T-shirt and tidied the bedroom where she and Timmy had slept.

She had no intention of going into Logan's room, but as she passed the half-opened door, an irresistible curiosity forced her to peek in.

White, off-white, pale blues and grays, the room shimmered with sunlight and soft morning breezes. She took a step in, then another, knowing she was invading a private space, but deriving too much pleasure from the trespassing to stop.

Logan had already made his bed, a long king-size affair set into a bay of windows. Gingerly she sat on the edge of the mattress and smoothed her palm over the puffy gray-and-blue spread. The next moment she was fighting an image of Logan asleep on that spread, dark hair mussed, long muscular arms flung out in invitation.

She shot up off the bed as if it were about to explode and brushed away all evidence of her sitting there.

Still, she couldn't bring herself to leave just yet. She studied a bookcase that contained a varied collection of nonfiction works: politics, business, science. But oddly those were overbalanced by whole shelves of Greek and Roman classics. In Greek and Latin, no less.

Slowly she made her way to the adjoining bathroom, which still held the crisp spicy scent of Logan's shaving that morning. Bemused beyond rational explanation, she ran her fingers over the smooth walnut knob of his shaving brush and sniffed the scent of his soap in a thick white towel.

On the windowsill sat a portable tape player and, intrigued by what Logan might've been listening to as he'd shaved that morning, she pressed the "play" button. A smile slid over her lips when the room filled with the silky sounds of Nat King Cole singing "Unforgettable."

Footsteps sounded in the hall, and Suzanna lunged to turn off the music. Her heart was palpitating and her cheeks blazed.

But the footsteps didn't belong to Logan, who she thought might've returned to the house for something he'd forgotten. The steps were Timmy's.

Still, Suzanna felt mortified. This behavior was so unlike her! She rewound the tape, wiped imagined fingerprints from the sink and ran off to spend the rest of the morning with her nephew, as she should have been doing all along.

THE FOLLOWING afternoon Suzanna received a call from her lawyer.

"How have you been, Suzanna?" Ray Quinn asked. "*Where* have you been?"

She plopped into the wooden chair in her office and, taking a deep breath, proceeded to tell him.

"You're what?"

"Spending nights at Mattashaum."

The line hummed for a long tense moment.

"Let me explain," she added, and then did, but as sketchily as possible. There was no need to overcomplicate matters by telling Ray about how well she and Logan were getting along.

But even while her words were spare, her mind filled with lush images: of her racing to Mattashaum last evening in order to share dessert with Logan and Timmy, a Black Forest cheesecake she'd absconded with from the shop; of their walk on the beach where they'd kicked through the surf and later sat in the shelter of a dune until the stars came out, listening to Logan tell tall tales about his colonial ancestors.

Ray breathed a gusty sigh. "Strange," he mumbled. "This is very strange. Be careful, Suzanna."

"Of course. Were you calling for a particular reason?"

"Yes, as a matter of fact. Your first interview with the court investigator is slated for two weeks this Monday."

Suzanna's mouth dried. Her first interview. The guardianship fight. Suddenly the images that had been filling her mind dissolved under the harsh light of reality.

"I'd like you to come by my office sometime soon so we can review the questions you're most likely going to be asked. I'll help you rehearse your answers."

"Is that necessary?"

"Absolutely. Another thing we've got to do is work on your financial profile."

"My what?"

"Finances. Ways of increasing your income, or at least making you look better on paper."

"What did you have in mind?" Apprehension prickled the back of her neck.

"Well, I was wondering if maybe you could raise the rent you charge your tenants."

Suzanna opened her mouth, but he went on before she could voice an objection.

"Another thought I had—is it possible for you to shift your catering business into a higher gear?"

"I . . . I'm already doing that. Logan—"

"Wonderful. Tell me all about it when you stop by. Here's one other thought, just a little something to mull over." He paused, and Suzanna sensed real hesitancy in the silence.

"What?"

"A rose-covered cottage in the suburbs."

"A what?"

"I'm not saying you actually have to move, just make the right noises. Look Suzanna, the Bradfords got you on the life-style issue. That's obviously their strength and your weakness—and the area you have to concentrate on be-tween now and the final hearing."

She dropped her forehead to her palm and sighed. "I know."

"Okay. Good. So we'll work on it."

Listlessly Suzanna opened her appointment calendar and they agreed on a time to meet.

"Buck up, Suzanna. We've only just begun to fight."

Yes, but so have the Bradfords, she thought dismally as she hung up the phone.

DESPITE THE ONGOING guardianship battle, the week passed in deepening harmony. That was due in large measure to the fact that neither Suzanna nor Logan let the subject arise in conversation. Their schedules meshed with surprising ease, and Timmy seemed to flourish under the new arrangement.

But then, Suzanna hadn't run into Collin, either, not since that awful afternoon in the yard with him and Cecily and the nanny. She was certain that if he knew she was sleeping at Logan's—Logan assured her he didn't know—her life would be far from harmonious, and each time she drove down the

Bradford lane, her heart pounded in fear that she'd come bumper-to-bumper with the old goat himself.

Labor Day weekend was extraordinarily busy at the shop, too busy for her to spend any time at Mattashaum. Suzanna was touched to tears, which she hid very badly, when Logan brought Timmy by on Sunday for a visit.

But the visit was short, and her pleasure turned to anger when Logan informed her he had an afternoon clambake to get to—at Cecily's.

"Are you taking Timmy, too?"

"Naturally."

Suzanna tossed a garden salad so viciously she feared even the carrots were getting bruised.

Logan leaned against the counter, watching her. "Timmy's feeling a lot more comfortable with me, and he seems to be taking the visits with his grandfather in stride. I thought he might be ready to start getting to know Cecily, too. What do you think?"

Suzanna dumped the salad into a large plastic container and slapped on the lid so hard the container cracked. She glared at Logan as if it was *his* fault. "It's only been a week. I think you're pushing your luck."

"Think so?"

"Isn't that what I just said?"

"Okay, okay. I won't take him to Cecily's."

Suzanna slumped with relief—until he added, "What are your thoughts on my father's housekeeper baby-sitting to-night? As you reminded me, Cecily and I haven't gone out much recently and we were thinking of taking in a movie after her clambake."

Suzanna pitched the salad into the cooler and slammed the door shut.

"Timmy seems to be quite comfortable with Mrs. Travis," Logan continued. "He chats up a storm with her whenever we pay a visit to the main house."

"So, have her baby-sit. Why ask me?"

Logan's sharp gray eyes traveled over her. "What is the matter with you, Suzanna?"

She swallowed, braced her hands on the sink and took a deep breath. She was acting ridiculous. So what if she and Timmy had spent a full week with Logan without Cecily intruding? That didn't give her the right to start believing Cecily would never be there. Cecily and Logan were engaged, for heaven's sake. Logan was going to marry her. He planned to make her Timmy's stepmother. Suzanna knew that; she'd always known that.

"Fine, go to your movie and have Mrs. Travis baby-sit. I like her, too," she replied in a small resigned voice. "And Logan? Thanks for including me in the decision."

As Suzanna embarked on her second week of staying at Mattashaum—and the thought of Cecily's becoming Timmy's stepmother took bitter root—she vowed to focus all her attention on strengthening her business and winning the guardianship case. To that end, she expanded her menu, placed ads with an upscale slant in several newspapers and, because response was immediate, was compelled to hire a new part-time helper.

She visited a real-estate office and, casting aside her feelings of awkwardness and guilt, pretended to be looking for a single-family home in the suburbs. While she was there, she also put Harris's studio on the market, a task she hadn't had the time or emotional energy for after the accident.

Clearing out the apartment he and her sister had lived in had been about all she could handle then. With the studio sold, she'd be able to close the equity loan she'd taken on her house.

That week she also met with her lawyer and learned how to phrase her responses when she was investigated to avoid saying anything that might be used against her.

Yes, indeed. From now on all her attention was going to be focused on winning Timmy back. That was all that really mattered.

But on Monday Logan brought a light aluminum canoe over from the main house just so she'd have something she was able to paddle around the pond by herself. That evening he let her row him and Timmy out to Elephant Rock where they built a small fire and toasted marshmallows.

And Tuesday morning he stayed home from the factory, and they picked wild blueberries and made blueberry ice cream and thick Belgian waffles, which they both agreed was a thoroughly improper lunch, but ate so much their stomachs hurt.

And on Wednesday Logan and Timmy picked her up at the shop so they wouldn't waste any time getting to the amusement park. It was there, while they were laughing at their reflections in the fun-house mirror, waving and bobbing to alter the distortions, that she realized she hadn't laughed so uninhibitedly in years. Logan, too, looked different. Younger. Carefree. And she thought, *We need this. We both need this badly.*

By Thursday evening Suzanna finally faced the fact that keeping her mind on business while she was with Logan took more concentration than she was capable of. Even when they weren't doing anything of particular interest, just folding laundry or reading in the living room after Timmy was asleep, Suzanna was aware of a new excitement in her blood, an exhilaration that blinded her to the issues she knew were so vital. In their place was Logan. He filled her senses and crowded her dreams, even when, in reality, he was ever so careful not to do anything to encourage her fascination.

On the contrary, Logan showed remarkable restraint. He called Cecily every evening that week, always with Suzanna in hearing range, and ended those calls with a whispered "Love you." On two of those evenings he even went to visit Cecily. And still Suzanna's awareness of him continued to grow—until her mouth went dry when he merely walked into a room, until her knees quaked when he handed her something and their fingers accidentally brushed, until standing next to him, she practically heard the electricity snapping across the distance from his arm to hers.

By Saturday night Suzanna was sitting at the kitchen table in Logan's house with her head in her hands and despair in her heart. Logan had left an hour ago to take Cecily to a party, and she had been sitting here ever since, feeling abandoned and burning with jealousy.

She slumped forward until her forehead touched the cool tabletop and moaned, "You're in deep, deep trouble, Keating."

A car engine purring to a stop caused her to sit bolt upright. A door slammed and a moment later a knock sounded on the kitchen door.

"Hello in there." The voice was feminine and light. "Logan?"

Suzanna belted her bathrobe over the nightgown she'd changed into after Logan had left and stared at the door, bewildered. The voice sounded curiously familiar. Her bewilderment increased a thousandfold when the door opened and Cecily popped her smooth blond head into the room.

"Logan?" she called again. When her eyes found Suzanna, she froze, then shoved the door wide. "What are *you* doing here?"

Suzanna rose slowly from her chair. "I might ask the same of you, Cecily."

"I don't have to explain my comings and goings to you. I'm Logan's fiancée." Even though Cecily was shorter than Suzanna, she still appeared to be looking down her nose at her. "Speaking of Logan, where is he?"

Suzanna frowned. Something mighty strange was going on here. "Out," she replied simply.

"And you're here ... ?"

"Baby-sitting."

Cecily took in Suzanna's attire with a clearly derisive sneer. "I find that hard to believe. You're the last person Logan would hire to baby-sit."

"He hasn't hired me. We've decided—"

"Did you sneak in here?" Cecily's look was becoming frostier by the second. "Are you trying to make a play for Logan or something? Isn't it enough that your sister got—"

"I told you, I'm baby-sitting."

"Dressed in pajamas?" Cecily laughed. "I don't know what your game is, Miss Keating, but I want you out of here."

"My game, Miss Knight, is simply to help Timmy adjust to living here. Surely Logan told you about what happened last week. The fit Timmy had when I tried to leave?"

Cecily's face fell.

"That's when Logan asked me to start sleeping over. But of course, you would know this already, you being Logan's fiancée." Suzanna placed a slightly mocking emphasis on the last phrase. "Surely he would've discussed such an important development with you."

Cecily looked stricken as she searched for a way to back-pedal out of the jam she'd put herself in. "Well, of course. Sure he did," she stammered, and Suzanna knew that Logan hadn't. Not a word.

That same moment, it hit her—what was odd about this visit, what was odd about Logan's relationship with this woman. It hit her like a lightning bolt, although Suzanna didn't betray her insight by so much as a muscle twitch. After all, she might be wrong.

On the other hand, she might be right, and suddenly she wanted to take Cecily's delicate well-dressed shoulders and shake a confession out of her. But she wouldn't. Oh, no. She would wait until a different set of shoulders presented themselves for shaking.

"Well, don't expect this living arrangement to last," Cecily said with more animosity than Suzanna had realized she harbored. "In fact, I was planning to discuss terminating it with Logan this very night."

Suzanna told herself she shouldn't direct her anger at Cecily, but hell, Cecily had been party to the deception, too.

If there was a deception, she reminded herself. That still needed confirmation.

Suzanna pulled out a chair. "Well, why don't you have a seat and wait for him to get back? It shouldn't be more than a couple of hours. He's out on a date."

She watched Cecily's expression like a hawk—and wasn't disappointed.

"A d-date?"

"Yes. By the way, it's supposed to be with you. A pity. You must've just missed each other."

Cecily's cheeks went from red to such an alarming white Suzanna almost felt sorry for her. Almost.

"You're going to rue this day," Cecily threatened, raising an overly dramatic fist. Then she spun on her heel and stormed off, leaving Suzanna with too much anger of her own to care.

She was waiting in the shadows of the living room when Logan returned. "How was your evening?" she asked.

He jumped a foot and gasped.

She grinned, pleased that retribution had already begun.

"Fine. What are you doing sitting here in the dark?" He switched on a lamp.

"On the contrary, I've been sitting here in the light—finally." She watched him scowl in puzzlement but didn't explain. "And how is Cecily?"

"Fine. She's fine."

Suzanna could take no more. She launched herself off the sofa and marched toward him, her nightclothes flapping like the robes of an avenging angel. "How *dare* you look at me so innocently while you're lying through your teeth. Cecily was *here* tonight." Logan gave a start. "That's right. Here. So you can drop your pitiful charade. I'm on to you, Bradford. It's over."

Instead of the hangdog repentant she expected him to become, Logan folded his arms across his broad chest, his gray eyes took on a hard glitter, and his teeth flashed in an infuriating grin. "Well," he drawled, "will you look at you!"

"Damn right, look at me. I'm mad, Logan. Furious."

Still smiling, he slowly loosened his tie, a familiar movement that suddenly struck her as terribly seductive. "That wouldn't be because you've been jealous as hell all week and now you realize your agonizing was unnecessary?"

"Of all the insufferable, arrogant... I have not been jealous! The idea is absurd."

"Okay, then what is it?" he asked, unbuttoning the top button of his shirt. "What's got you so angry about Cecily and me not being engaged?"

"You don't know?" she shrieked to the rafters. "You lied, Logan. In front of a judge."

He scratched his head, studied the carpet, but never relinquished his infernal amusement. "The engagement was my lawyers' suggestion, not mine. I said it was dicey business right from the start. Does that win me any points?"

"Augh! You slime!" Her hands balled into fists as she stalked closer. "You toad!" One of her fists landed on his arm.

"Hey, that hurt."

"Good." She punched him again. "You deserve much worse. That lie of yours helped sway the judge. It helped you take Timmy away from me."

Holding his battered arm, he asked, "Are you done?"

"No." But she could feel her lower lip trembling. "How could you do that? How could you play so dirty?"

"I like to win." His diamond-bright eyes still laughed at her.

"Logan! What's got into you? How can you find such hurtful deceit funny?"

"Not the deceit, Suzanna. I'm truly sorry about that." He sobered enough for her to see he meant what he said. "Right now I'm acting like a pie-eyed jackass because the deception's over. It's quite a relief."

"I'm sure," she agreed with mincing sarcasm. "Now you can stop phoning Cecily just for my benefit." She watched his reaction carefully to see if he'd squirm.

"Yes. That certainly was a nuisance."

She gasped. "Even *that* you're trying to hide?"

His head tilted, eyes lit with deepening fascination. "Exactly what am I trying to hide now?"

Infuriated by his refusal to be thrown off balance, she stomped a foot. "The fact that you never called Cecily at all! Jeez, Logan, didn't you feel like a moron saying things like, 'How was your tennis match, sweetie?' when all the while the answering machine at your factory was saying back to you, 'Thank you for calling Bradford Energy Systems. You've reached us after hours, but if you'll leave your name and number—' "

Logan howled with laughter. "How the devil did you figure that one out?"

"Simple. After Cecily left tonight, I remembered that you'd called her earlier and that it was the last call made from that phone. So I hit the 'redial' button and, bingo, 'Thank you for calling Bradford Energy Systems . . .' "

"You're amazing." Logan shook his head and smiled.

She folded her arms tight. "No, I'm infuriated."

He stared at her a long uncomfortable moment. "And I'm not engaged."

"I know!" She tossed up her hands in exasperation.

But as his steady stare continued to burn into her, as his lopsided grin turned devilish, Suzanna grew unsure of herself. When he took a step toward her, she instinctively took a step back.

"Don't you understand? I'm free, Suzanna, and I'm finally able to say it." He took another step—and she backed up one. "I'm free. Not engaged. To Cecily or anyone else."

Suzanna felt pinned by his gaze, a helpless doe caught in the beam of a headlight. "Why d-do you keep repeating the obvious?" Her voice was breathy, the strength to speak deserting her.

"Because I love the sound of it." He continued to stalk her, step for step, until her heart was hammering high in her throat and her brain was a frenzied blank.

"Do you know what the best part of not being engaged is?" he asked, his low voice wrapping around her like a spell. She shook her head—just as her left heel hit the wall. She let out a little gasp.

Logan's grin faded as he planted his hands on either side of her head, corralling her to the wall. "The best part . . ."

Mesmerized, Suzanna watched his lips shape the words, remembered their softness, felt his voice resonate deep inside her.

"The best part is I don't have to feel guilty when I do this." He closed his hands over her shoulders and slowly pulled her away from the wall across the few inches that divided them. When their bodies met, she drew in a soft hissing breath.

"Or this," Logan murmured. His lips were like hot silk on her forehead, on her eyelids, on her cheek. Suzanna was reeling in a haze of heat and stardust by the time he reached her chin.

And finally he arrived at her lips, breathing, "Or this," just before his mouth closed over hers.

Don't, Suzanna tried to say. At least she meant to. But under Logan's tender assault, her resistance wilted. *She* wilted, forgetting everything they had been arguing about. She wrapped her arms around his neck and returned his kiss with an abandon that would've embarrassed her except that she was enjoying it too much. Immediately she felt a response. Logan pressed his hands across her back, folding her closer, deepening his kiss, which, she was quite sure, was like nothing else on earth.

Yes! her whole being sang. This was definitely the best part of his not being engaged. And yes, she had been jealous; she'd been green with it.

When Logan finally lifted his head, his breathing was ragged. "Suzanna, Suzanna." He closed his eyes and tucked her against his thudding heart, resting his chin on the crown of her head. "If only you knew how hard this week has been, having you here and not being able to touch you, knowing if I did, you'd think I was cheating on Cecily."

She clutched his shirt, still shivering, still trying to cope with the myriad explosions he'd set off inside her. She wanted to tell him she had been miserable, too, but already fear was snaking through her happiness. "Logan, what are we doing?" she cried in a hoarse whisper.

He stroked her head, his fingers twining in her long hair. "Complicating matters incredibly, I'd say." He tilted her face up and smiled.

But she couldn't smile back. She pressed closer, soaking up the heat of his body, absorbing his heartbeat, his scent, his strength. She wanted this moment to go on forever. But even now, she knew it couldn't. Reality was going to intrude.

"This is an impossible situation, you realize that, don't you?" she whispered.

He grew serious, moving away from her a little, and after a pensive pause answered, "Yes."

Suzanna's heart plummeted. That wasn't the answer she had been looking for.

"I think, for everyone's sake we'd better call it a night," he said, turning to stare out the windows.

"Yes, I guess we should."

"See you in the morning, Suzanna," he said, but she was already hurrying to her room.

CHAPTER TEN

THE NEXT AFTERNOON Logan received a call from Collin requesting he come to the main house to look over some documents their attorneys had mailed.

"Can't it wait till tomorrow?" Logan watched Suzanna and Timmy threading their way through a spongy bog of cattails on a far rim of the pond, gathering a bouquet. It was a still, unseasonably hot day, and he wanted to be out there with them enjoying it before autumn settled in for good.

"Afraid not," Collin replied. "They look pretty important."

Logan pressed his fist against the window in controlled frustration. "Okay. I'll see you in a few minutes."

"Good. Oh, and bring the boy with you. I have something to show him."

Logan was reluctant to tear Timmy away from his explorations, but lately he'd noticed a change in Collin. Not much really—a certain clearness of eye, a slight lift in his voice. Nonetheless it was enough to gladden Logan's heart.

He found his father sitting in his study, a hunting rifle he hadn't used in several years lying across his spindly knees. The rifle cabinet was open and Logan wandered over, instinctively seeking out the .22-caliber Remington Collin had taught him to use when he was a boy.

"Whatcha doin', Grandpa?" Still a bit shy, Timmy sidled up to Collin cautiously.

"Cleaning and oiling my gun."

The child's eyes rounded at the word "gun" while his mouth gaped at the sight of it. "What...what you do with that gun?"

"I hunt, Timothy. Pheasant, rabbit, grouse. Oh, and ducks. That's my favorite kind of hunting." He raised the rifle to his eye, taking aim at phantom prey. "Someday, if you're a good boy, I'll take you with me. Would you like that?"

Timmy ground the toe of his sneaker into the Persian carpet. He seemed confused, and Logan could only imagine his contradictory feelings of aversion and fascination.

He turned from the cabinet. "Collin, for heaven's sake. He's only—"

"I know. Four years old." Collin chuckled. "I didn't mean *this* season."

Logan wasn't sure he wanted Timmy hunting *any* season, but it was still a joy to see his father looking forward to the future.

"Where are those papers you wanted me to look over?"

"On my desk," Collin said distractedly, his attention now bent on an album he was showing his grandson, snapshots of himself as a strapping younger man with his two handsome sons, taken during hunting seasons years ago.

Logan had only to glance at the documents to realize they were routine. He tossed them back on the desk. "Tim, could you give me and Grandpa a few minutes alone, please? Go see what Mrs. Travis is cooking up in the kitchen, okay?"

Once the boy skipped off, Logan voiced his suspicion. "What's this all about, Collin?"

Collin cut straight to the chase. "Cecily phoned me this morning." With Timmy gone, his eyes lost their warmth. "I was aware that the Keating girl was spending her mornings at your place, but Cecily informs me she's taken to staying there nights, too. Is that true?"

Logan returned his father's unflinching stare with one of his own, despite the sick feeling in his stomach. "Yes," he replied.

"Yes? Just as bold as brass you stand there and say yes?"

"Yes."

Collin flung the album aside. "Have you lost your mind?"

"For heaven's sake, Collin, what's the big deal?"

"I don't want her here, that's the big deal. She reminds me of that scheming avaricious sister of hers and the pain she caused our family. She distresses me, Logan." Collin rose from his chair and paced. "Her being around Timothy can't be doing him any good, either. Confusing him. Prolonging the separation process."

Logan listened to his father's impassioned words, opinions he himself had espoused—was it really just two weeks ago? Because those two weeks had been filled with getting to know Suzanna, he felt he'd traveled over whole continents of time. He now understood things about her and Tim, about vulnerability and mother love, that Collin didn't and never would. Or would he?

"I wish you knew how helpful she's been to me, settling Timmy in."

Collin snorted. "No doubt with personal gain in mind. Or have you forgotten that Timothy stands to inherit three million dollars?"

Logan pressed the bridge of his nose, fighting down his rising anger. "Father, listen to me. Suzanna isn't like that. Issues have blurred. If we were to go to court tomorrow, I'd be the first to say she's an integral part of Timmy's life. And I think—no, I know the time has come for us to bend."

Collin stopped his pacing and his face suffused with color. "I will not bend!"

"But your grandson's emotional well-being depends on her."

Collin eyed him through narrowed burning slits. "If he needs a maternal influence, he should spend more time with Cecily."

Logan trembled with the effort to control his temper. "I figured we'd get around to her again."

"Well? What about Cecily?"

"I don't see the point."

"But you're engaged."

Logan cast his father a look of impatience.

"All right, so it's an arrangement we set up to suit our purposes, but sooner or later it would've happened, anyway. We both know you and Cecily are inevitable."

"I hate to disappoint you, but Cecily and I are not inevitable. *Finished* is what we are."

Collin's chest rose and fell with a rapidity that made Logan uneasy. "What do you mean, finished?"

"Over. Done with. Suzanna put two and two together. It was bound to happen. I'm a lousy liar, and she..." Logan suspected he smiled a little. "She's a very sharp woman."

"She knows?" Collin stopped at the sofa table, his fingers trembling as they reached for a gold cigarette case.

"Yes, she knows."

Collin cursed vehemently.

Logan went over to the table and pulled the cigarettes from his father's grip. "Sit down, Collin." He pressed the old man into a chair. "Calm down."

"I will not calm down. Do you realize the ammunition that girl now possesses to take into court?"

"Suzanna wouldn't do that. She isn't like that."

Collin glanced up sharply and every muscle of his body stilled. He didn't even breathe. "Damn you, Logan!" he finally burst forth. "She's gaining influence over you!" His color drained away until he slumped there looking old and frail.

Logan sat on the arm of Collin's chair and placed a hand on the old man's shoulder, saying nothing.

"Ah, son, what are you doing?" Collin implored sadly.

Logan swallowed. Whatever was blossoming between Suzanna and him he resisted sharing with Collin. "You're reading more into this than exists," he said, but he felt transparent.

Collin shook his white head, placed a hand over his son's knee and patted it as if in sympathy. "Son, a relationship with that girl is out of the question, if for no other reason than you come from different backgrounds. You have nothing in common. You know that. I know you do."

Logan cast his gaze aside, increasingly pensive.

"Oh, I understand how you may want to sleep with her. Don't look so shocked. I was young once, too, and she is a distracting female. But you've got to control those urges. Think, son, think. Remember your pride. When you've been at war with someone for five long years, you don't suddenly form a liaison with her, especially not that sort."

Logan heard the loving concern in his father's voice, and because it touched him, he allowed himself to consider the sense in what Collin was saying.

"A romantic liaison," his father continued, "is the most vulnerable sort there is. Who knows? She might even be leading you on purposely, to make a fool of you, to soften you so you won't fight her as hard as you could."

Quiet and grim, Logan pondered the possibility. A weight settled on his chest.

"Be on your guard, especially now." Collin smiled wanly, fatherly regard shining in his eyes. "Women may be glorious creatures, but you can't trust a single damn one."

Logan lurched to his feet and walked to the window. Outside, the afternoon was thickening with dark gray clouds. He felt like a barometer, the pressure bearing down on him, crushing the air from his lungs.

"As I said, there's nothing going on between me and Suzanna."

"Then you'll tell her she isn't needed here every day? You'll not let her stay overnight?"

Logan dragged a hand down his troubled face. Collin was right of course. Suzanna *was* staying over well beyond the point where she was needed. "Yes," he promised simply.

"Good, good." Collin nodded. "I've always been able to count on you, Logan."

ON THE FAR SIDE of Mattashaum, Suzanna pushed the lightweight canoe into the water and hopped in. Her T-shirt clung to her ribs in the humid heat, and her instincts told her she'd be far better off lounging on the patio with a glass of iced tea.

Unfortunately she'd awakened this morning with a determination to prepare a seafood stew for supper. Recently Logan had been reminiscing about a bouillabaisse he'd had in France and never forgotten, and no amount of discomfort was going to keep her from her purpose.

She beached the canoe on Elephant Rock Island, then with rake and bucket in hand, splashed out to the quahog bed where she and Logan had dug two weeks earlier.

There she paused, leaning on her rake, and gazed across the leaden pond toward Logan's house, seeing Logan in her mind's eye, instead. Simultaneously an upswell of emotion threatened to undo her.

She'd never felt so drawn to a man before. Just the thought of how he'd kissed her last night made heat spill deep into her, warming her right to her fingertips. She closed her eyes, riding the shivery sensations until they subsided somewhat.

When she reopened her eyes, bittersweet sadness touched her smile. She'd waited all her life to find someone who could move her so, had all but given up hope of ever finding him, and here he was. Here he was, and like a child with her nose pressed against a toy-shop window, the only thing she could do was dream.

She and Logan would never be able to get together. Reasons abounded. There were family animosities, their disparate backgrounds and the legal battle that was fast approaching. But if she were truly honest she'd have to admit that at the base of all her reasons was fear. It was a vague sort of fear, more a foreboding. Yet the closer she got to Logan the worse it became, until now, today, it seemed everywhere.

Inexplicably her skin crawled.

Standing knee-deep in water, Suzanna raised her eyes and turned a slow half circle. The landscape had turned gray and was darkening even as she watched. Suddenly she didn't want to be here anymore. A malevolence seemed to be rising into the atmosphere, seeping from the ground of Mattashaum itself.

Overhead, pushed by a wind she hadn't noticed before, a flock of birds tumbled eastward. Trees dipped and twisted, their leaves turning over and surrendering.

Suzanna turned again, to the west, toward the main house, and her breath stalled. A bank of towering clouds was riding toward her, dragging ragged gray veils from their black underbellies. With them raced their shadow, casting untimely dusk across the point, and then the ocean, and now the dunes.

Even as Suzanna watched, a blinding sword of lightning scissored down from the sky.

LOGAN DROVE SLOWLY down the lane to his house, so slowly he actually rolled to a stop, staring ahead blankly, lost in his thoughts.

Timmy had asked to stay behind because Mrs. Travis was baking his favorite cookies, chocolate chip, and Collin was unearthing more mementos from a trunk. Logan appreciated the break. He needed some time alone with Suzanna to discuss their relationship.

He gripped the top of the steering wheel and dropped his chin to his knuckles. Cooling things with Suzanna wasn't going to be easy. He ached even now, just thinking about her. But Collin was right. Logan had begun playing at something he never should have allowed to start, and before it got any more complicated, he had to end it.

Not that he believed Suzanna was purposely leading him on, as Collin claimed. His distrust of her motives was gone. No, what had him worried now was precisely the opposite—the genuineness and sheer strength of their feelings for each other.

What did he intend to do with this attraction? He had to look ahead to eventualities. He'd never been a man to take relationships lightly or irresponsibly, but was he ready to follow this one to its natural conclusion? Hardly. Pain lay in that direction, complications so dreadful his brain shut down at the thought....

Logan's attention was jogged back to the present when the world beyond his windshield flashed with lightning. He peered up at the sky through the arching branches of trees. A few seconds later thunder rolled and clapped with a deep boom. The forecast had warned of a cold front moving in to clear away this humid heat, and all day he'd felt the pressure building. He put his car in motion just as rain began to fall.

SUZANNA'S FINGERS dug into the shale at the base of Elephant Rock while another boom of thunder cracked overhead. Lord, what a storm! She'd never seen anything like it. It had come on so fast, too. Her only consolation was that Timmy was with Logan and didn't have to endure this nightmare with her.

She was certain she'd be all right, though. She'd realized right off that the aluminum canoe was a natural conductor of electricity and had pushed it out onto the pond. She'd also put as much distance as possible between herself and the island's lone tree.

The thunder was heart shaking, the lightning flashed so fast it seemed intent on burning down the sky, but lying flat in the lee of the big rock, she felt relatively safe. The rain was cold, beating the warmth out of the air, and she was shivering, but she hadn't a single doubt she would pull through. She had to.

When the latest crash of thunder faded, she turned her head, cushioning it on her folded arms, and squinted through the heavy sheets of rain toward the cottage on the hill. How she wished she was back there now, sitting by a fire, wrapped in a warm robe, sipping tea—

Abruptly her thoughts scattered. She braced herself on one elbow unable—unwilling—to believe what she was seeing. The old wooden rowboat was in the water, and Logan was rowing toward her like a man possessed, pulling the oars so hard the heavy boat lurched with each stroke.

"Oh, God, no!" The words left her lips in an anguished cry. *What are you doing?* Already the air smelled singed, and in the distance sirens wailed. *Where is your common sense?* Her heart drummed against her ribs, and despite the chill in her bones she felt hot with terror. She sat up, watching him, her body pulling with his efforts, her spirit willing him to outrun the next deadly bolt.

Lightning forked down from the warring clouds, bleaching the entire landscape for a few long flickering seconds. A tree up by the cottage split and smoldered.

But Logan was still rowing, his rhythm unbroken.

Suzanna pressed her clasped hands to her mouth to stop the cry that wanted to escape. *Hurry. Please, hurry!* she prayed, glancing from Logan to the oak tree ten yards away from her, the only two projections on all these watery acres. In that instant, her entire attention was fixed on Logan, on the oak, and the game of Russian roulette they were playing with the cosmos.

With one last heave, the boat scraped up on the shore.

"Logan!" Suzanna leapt to her feet, swallowing her sobs.

"Suzanna!" Logan ran to her and wrapped her in an embrace that lifted her off her feet. He held her so tightly she could barely breathe.

"Come, get down," she managed nonetheless.

They flung themselves to the sodden sand, Suzanna on her side with her back to the rock, Logan shielding her with his body. His shirt and trousers were soaked through, but he still radiated a warmth, generated by his strenuous exertions.

"You're all right?" he asked, smoothing back her wet hair, his eyes devouring her features.

"Yes, I'm fine. But you... Oh, Logan, it's a miracle you weren't struck." At just the thought she held him close, burying her face in his neck. "You must've realized how dangerous it was."

"Not for a second. When I got to the house and discovered you weren't there, I stopped thinking and started running on adrenaline." As if experiencing the fright all over again, he kissed her cheek, her brow, her ear—hard quick kisses that spoke of desperation. "And then, through my binoculars, I saw you here, flat on the ground, facedown and unmoving, and I thought..." He let the sentence trail off and showered her with kisses again. "All I knew was I had to get to you."

"Oh, Logan," she said with a laugh, even as tears burned in her eyes. "I'm not as dumb as I look. I was careful. But you! Don't ever, ever do anything so foolhardy again." She ran urgent hands through his rain-heavy hair, down his strong muscled back and up to his neck, wanting to assure herself he was all right—and would be so forever. *Because I don't know how I'd go on if anything ever happened to you,* she thought.

Logan gazed deep into her eyes. Did he see her thoughts in them? she wondered. Did he see the love?

And she *did* love him, she now realized clearly. When she'd seen him rowing toward her through the storm, everything in her life had telescoped to that one basic truth. She loved him, and all the reasons she shouldn't fell away to nothing.

"Then, don't you ever get yourself into this sort of trouble again," he murmured, his face growing serious. "Because I will come to your rescue, every time." The next moment he was kissing her, a tender impassioned kiss that seemed to have more to do with the sealing of promises than with physical desire—although when Logan raised his head, Suzanna saw that desire shone in his heavy-lidded eyes, as well.

She swallowed, recognizing a matching need in herself. With a boldness she'd never felt before, she hooked her arms around his neck and drew him to her again. This time when they kissed, desire coursed between them undisguised. Lips parted, mouths fit possessively, and Logan tasted of her hungrily, sending hot shivers to her innermost core. She curled into his heat, impatience quickening her breath.

Logan nipped at her full lower lip, kissed her eyelids, then returned to her waiting mouth, plundering it until she felt as if every cell of her body had caught fire. She flung her arms over her head, both languid and vibrantly alive, and Logan acknowledged her surrender with a low throaty growl. He ran his hands, hard and slow, up the length of her wet arms, until their palms met and their fingers interlocked.

"You can't imagine what you do to me." With their lips parted and brushing, he breathed the words into her mouth.

"Oh, yes, I can," she returned fervently. "Logan, this has never happened to me before." She closed her eyes, shuddering as he traced the outline of her lips with the tip of his tongue.

"To me, either," he whispered just before his mouth closed over hers. It was several minutes before she could speak, and by then she'd very nearly lost her train of thought.

"But you're older, Logan, more experienced. I'd understand if... I mean, you must have had women who..." Her cheeks bloomed with embarrassment.

With eyes that smoldered, Logan stared directly into hers and shook his head. "Never. Never like you."

She melted under the ardor of his words. Her heart thumped wildly against his chest. "It frightens me, Logan."

"No, don't be frightened." He folded her closer, rocking her. "Don't."

That afternoon, lying entwined, Logan and Suzanna discovered a passion that was as wild as the storm crashing about them, and almost as mindless. Somehow, though, Logan managed to hang on to his wits. A cold gritty beach wasn't how he wanted Suzanna to remember the first time they made love. Oh, no. When they finally did take that momentous step, he would pull out all the stops—on comfort, on luxury, on romance.

When the storm finally passed, Logan rowed them back toward his house. Faint thunder rumbled in the eastern distances over Cape Cod, but from the west, bright sunlight slanted under the thinning veils of cloud. The air was cool and dry, the change in the weather marking also a change in the seasons.

He and Suzanna spoke little but smiled a lot, grins that lifted from some giddy well of newfound joy. They forgot that they were waterlogged, forgot their hair was matted with sand, forgot they shouldn't hug and kiss when the boat bumped the shore, or cling to each other as they climbed the path.

Only when they slid open the patio door and saw Collin sitting at the kitchen table did they remember to remember.

"Collin!" Logan dropped his arm from Suzanna's shoulders. "What are you doing here?"

His father pushed up slowly from the table, his all-seeing eyes moving icily from Logan to Suzanna. "Timothy became distressed by the storm and asked to be returned."

Suzanna stepped forward, alarmed. "Is he all right? Where is he?"

Collin's contempt was palpable as he stared at her. "Yes, he's fine. He's playing in his room." He turned his accusing gaze on Logan. "And how are you two?"

Instinctively Logan moved closer to Suzanna and curled his arm around her shoulders again. He saw Collin watching him—and was startled by the realization that he didn't care. "We're fine," he answered, then took a few minutes to sketch out what had happened.

Collin stood motionless through the narrative, not even a muscle twitch betraying what he was thinking. Logan wondered what he was going to say, how he would display his anger, but he was pleasantly surprised when Collin left without a single disparaging comment.

"Well!" Logan stared at the retreating automobile, dazed. "Well," he repeated, not knowing what else to say.

"He saw us, Logan. If not on the island, then when we were returning."

"No question about it." Logan turned to face her, wearing a befuddled half smile. "You know something, this may work out easier than I thought."

"Maybe." Suzanna walked into his upraised arms, but not for a minute did she really believe what she'd said.

CHAPTER ELEVEN

TWO BLISSFUL DAYS went by. Suzanna and Logan kept to their work schedules as arranged, and she continued to sleep over. Everything was the same as before—but different. Their awareness of each other had leapt in intensity to a degree where nights spent under the same roof, but apart, throbbed with a longing that became impossible to endure. The kisses and embraces they shared, meant to slake their need, served only to fan its fire.

Quite frankly, Suzanna adored the situation. She'd fallen in love with Logan, and although they'd never actually spoken the words, she felt he loved her, too, or at least was well on his way. They'd crossed a threshold of some sort, and she was happy.

Still, when she was alone, as she was on the third morning after the storm, she let herself acknowledge that they were living in an uneasy calm. They hadn't heard from Collin since he'd driven off, but neither had they forgotten him.

She was watering the geraniums on the sunny south deck when the sound of an approaching car drew her attention. She put the watering can down and crossed to the steps, drying her hands on her shirttails. But her curiosity gave way to dread when she saw who was coming to call.

"Mr. B-Bradford," she stammered, watching him approach, his cane stabbing the path with each step. "Are you here to see Logan?" Her temples pounded. Alone with the old man, she felt oddly defenseless.

He merely stared at her, his hands gripping the top of the cane. Suzanna was thankful Timmy was inside absorbed in his favorite cartoon show.

With a hard narrowing of his eyes, Collin finally said, "We have to talk."

"Would you c-care to sit?"

Again he didn't answer. Apparently he didn't intend to respond to anything she said. "I suppose you think you're very clever, Miss Keating."

"I beg your pardon?"

"The way you've insinuated yourself into my son's life."

Suzanna gulped, but the lump in her throat refused to dissolve.

"Well, missy, I'm here to tell you your scheme won't work."

She'd so wanted to believe her happiness with Logan was real and lasting, but part of her had always known she was just playing at Cinderella. Collin's resentment of her was unrelenting, his possessiveness toward his family too blind.

"I admit that Logan and I have grown close, Mr. Bradford, but it was hardly a scheme."

"Don't insult me with your lies. I know what you're up to. You think if you snare my son, you'll win the boy, too, no contest." The old man laughed, a dry raspy sound like winter reeds in a cold wind. "I have to give you credit. I didn't think your ambition was so far-reaching."

"What are you talking about?" Now she was truly confused.

"Money, Miss Keating. The stuff that makes the world go round. I figured the boy's three million was enough, but I underestimated you. Evidently you're in this for the jackpot."

His meaning finally came clear, and Suzanna gasped. "You think I'm after Logan's money?"

"His and the boy's. But really, Miss Keating, don't you think this particular ploy is getting a little stale?"

She suspected she was frowning in puzzlement again. His expression turned hard with impatience.

"Your sister thought a clever marriage would fix her for life, too, didn't she? But it didn't work, and you'd better believe it's not going to work now."

"I'm not after anyone's money. The only thing I've ever wanted—"

"My family will not be used. Do you understand?"

It hurt to hear him speak so harshly, to know he thought so little of her. Despite everything, Collin was still a man she could love simply because he was Logan's father. Yet she could see nothing she said was going to soften his view, and so she hardened her own.

"What exactly is your point, Mr. Bradford?"

"I want you out of our lives—permanently. You're to get off this property and stop pursuing Logan."

"But I have visitation rights. I come here to see my nephew with the court's full blessing."

"Do you actually think I care? This is my home and I don't want you here. Moreover, I want you to drop this challenge for custody."

"Drop the...? You're telling me...?" She was flabbergasted.

"You heard me. I don't want even *that* much contact with you."

"This isn't about you and me!" she shouted. But a cold stream of fear suddenly sluiced down her spine. Perhaps this really was about her and him, after all. "You have no right," she protested in a voice that strained to be heard.

"I have every right," Collin boasted.

She swallowed convulsively. "And what if I don't comply with your outrageous demands? What if I continue to fight for guardianship?"

Collin's thin lips curled. "Then prepare to lose everything you own, missy."

She stared at him in disbelief, her breathing shallow and rapid.

"Think about it. Think of the consequences if you persist. In the first place, you're going to lose the suit. That's a given. Not only will you not have Timmy but you'll be out money—thousands of dollars is my estimation. Going to court is a costly proposition, and I plan to drag out these proceedings as long as possible." His animosity was grinding. "But if by some fluke you do win the boy, I guarantee it'll be an empty victory."

Suzanna's skin began to crawl with intimation. "H-how can winning him be empty?"

Collin leaned in. "If you become my grandson's guardian, I'm afraid he will never see a penny of his money."

His pronouncement hit like a physical blow. "You'd do that? Withhold his rightful inheritance?"

"Without a bat of an eye, and don't you ever doubt it."

Suzanna shook her head. "How typical of you. How predictable. Oh, Mr. Bradford, when will you ever learn? I don't care about Timmy's money. At least I'd have *him*."

"And what would he have, Miss Keating?" He leveled her with his stare. "Do you really believe you're worth three million dollars?"

She felt her resolve sway with uncertainty. "But my love, my care..."

"Is your loving care so precious and unique that it justifies the deprivation you'll cause Timothy? Are you that arrogant? That egotistical?"

Suzanna stared off toward the ocean, thinking. Maybe Collin was right. Maybe she *was* serving her own interests, not Timmy's, feeding a selfish need to feel indispensable. She sighed heavily, wishing Logan was here.

Logan.

Immediately she felt more hopeful. Collin was painting a scenario that Logan would never allow to happen. These past few weeks they'd come so far....

"I wish I'd made the effort to visit you," she said, "so you could've gotten to know me the way Logan has. He and I have bridged many of the problems we faced in court. You're speaking about animosities that don't even exist anymore." She wrung her hands, wanting to tell him she loved his son, but she could see from his stormy gray eyes that she'd said too much already.

"Leave my son alone. This is the last time I'm warning you. Get out of his life and stay out."

She met his glare, and he met hers, neither backing down.

"And if I don't?" Suzanna knew she was pushing, but she needed to know just how far Collin intended to go. Besides, what else could he possibly threaten her with?

"If you don't, Miss Keating, and if for some reason my son is foolish enough to follow in his brother's footsteps—" he paused, heightening the tension "—then I'll have no choice. Logan will never—and I solemnly mean never—inherit Mattashaum from me."

Suzanna felt the color drain from her face. "You can't mean that."

"Oh, can't I? And by Mattashaum I don't mean just the property. That includes all the investments and business holdings in my estate, and they are considerable."

Investments and business holdings didn't concern Suzanna at the moment, however. But Mattashaum did! "This property has been in your family for almost three centuries. Who would you leave it to if not Logan?"

"I'd sell it to developers and give the money to charity. Developers have been hounding me for years."

"But Logan loves Mattashaum, its history, its environment." Tears burned in her throat. "Don't you understand? People draw their energy from all sorts of sources. This happens to be his. How could you even contemplate selling it to developers? That would kill your son."

Collin's expression went calm with satisfaction. "I'm glad you understand, Miss Keating. Glad you understand."

For several minutes after Collin had left, Suzanna stood motionless on the deck, immobilized by his ultimatum. That he had the power to make good on his threats she had no doubt. While he'd relinquished most of the running of Mattashaum and its holdings to Logan, Collin had not relinquished ownership. Neither did she doubt he had the will to go forward on his threats. He'd done it before, to another son and to the girl who'd been audacious enough to love that son. Oh, yes, Collin would have his way.

Suzanna lifted her gaze to the landscape she'd grown to love, but misery blurred its beauty.

Collin had done it—put Logan in the same position as Harris was in five years ago. But somehow this felt worse. So much more was at stake.

What would Logan do? she wondered. What would be his choice? For a moment she let herself indulge in a romantic fantasy in which Logan laughed in defiance at Collin's ultimatum—and she came out the winner.

But the moment passed quickly. She moaned, dragging her hands down her anguished face. She wouldn't be able to live with herself knowing she had deprived Logan of Mattashaum.

Not that she really thought there was any danger of that happening. Logan would never be as foolhardy as Harris and give up everything just to be with the woman he loved. He was older, wiser, and far more attached to Mattashaum. But more importantly he'd never actually said he loved her, had he? That was the crux of the matter.

She stumbled into the house, Collin's parting comment returning to haunt her. The situation, he'd implied, was now in her hands. Completely. She nodded to herself, full understanding dawning. Logan needn't ever know about the ultimatum, needn't ever have to face such a painful choice.

Moreover, Suzanna didn't *want* him to. For whatever reason, he still loved his father, still respected him and went to extremes to excuse his behavior. She didn't want him to discover just how malicious Collin could be, would willingly be, even to Logan, his firstborn son. Now his only son. No child deserved such cruel disillusionment, especially someone who'd been as loyal as Logan.

She would leave—that was the solution. She would drop the guardianship suit and stop visiting Mattashaum just as Collin had suggested. The only difficult aspect of the plan would be convincing Logan that the decision was hers and that she was comfortable with it. Not just comfortable, enthusiastic. Immediately she knew she'd never be able to pull it off face-to-face.

A letter. Yes, that might work.

She found a box of stationery in the living-room desk and, sitting down, picked up a pen and began.

She kept the tone upbeat, explaining that she was dropping the fight because, coming to know him as she had, she now realized what an excellent parent he'd make. She admitted he was right; he *could* provide for Timmy better than she. She conceded that Timmy loved living here and seemed fully adjusted. She even added a paragraph about realizing she liked her freedom and wanted to use it to concentrate on her catering business, maybe even start traveling a bit.

The only point she refused to concede to Collin was dropping out of Timmy's life entirely. She didn't have to ever see Logan again or return to Mattashaum, but she wouldn't let Timmy grow up thinking she had abandoned him. In a postscript she informed Logan that he would be hearing from her lawyer to work out a visitation schedule. Collin wouldn't like it, but on this point she wouldn't back down.

When she was done, she sealed the letter in an envelope and propped it on the kitchen table where Logan was sure to find it. She called the main house and to her relief the housekeeper answered. When Suzanna explained that she had to leave, Mrs. Travis readily offered to come over to stay with Timmy until Logan got home. That done, Suzanna packed up her possessions, which were scattered about the house, all the while trying not to think. Whenever she did, the pain cut too deep.

Finally there was only one task remaining. She stood in the doorway of Timmy's room, watching him and his puppy tumbling on the carpeted floor, the cartoon show ignored.

"Tim?" She walked in and lowered the television's volume.

The child sat up, his hair sticking this way and that in disheveled clumps, his velvet-smooth cheeks aglow.

"Tim, I've got to go back to the city early today." She bit her lip. "And I won't be able to sleep here tonight."

Timmy blinked, digesting her message. "Okay," he replied cheerfully, reaching for a red ball Buddy had batted under the bed.

"I *will* see you soon, though."

The child smiled the most trusting smile she'd ever seen. "I know," he said. She thought her heart would break.

Just then the kitchen door opened and Mrs. Travis called a greeting. Suzanna swallowed her tears and squared her shoulders. It was time to leave.

LOGAN WHISTLED all the way home from the factory. He couldn't remember the last time he'd felt so alive or in tune with the universe. Sales were up, it was his favorite time of year, and more importantly, he had two very special people waiting for him at the house.

His car bounced down the lane too fast and came to a jerking stop by the door. Logan was grinning just at the thought of seeing Suzanna again. That full lush mouth. Those smoky green eyes. Her infectious laugh and buoyant spirit.

Suddenly Logan's grin faded. Her van was gone and in its place sat Mrs. Travis's dull blue Chevy. He told himself he had no cause to worry, but still, he took the steps all in one leap.

"Suzanna?" An edge of apprehension thinned his voice even before his gaze fell on the envelope.

"She's gone," Mrs. Travis called, coming through the living room. "She didn't explain, but there's a note."

He was already reading, his eyes racing in disbelief. What did she mean she was dropping the guardianship suit? Timmy meant more to her than her own life. "This doesn't make sense," he muttered.

He reread the letter, then went to stare out the window. A knot of guilt tightened under his ribs. He should have broached the issue with her, let her know that he no longer wished to fight but was hoping to work out a compromise. Instead, he'd avoided the subject as if it would go away all by itself. Did he think she was a mind reader?

"Damn!" He whirled toward the phone, intent on calling her. But then he paused. Her leaving so abruptly still didn't make sense. She would've had to be blind not to see how much he cared for her, a dolt not to realize that the game plan had changed. And Suzanna Keating was neither blind nor a dolt.

No, something else must have happened to cause this odd behavior. Something—or someone.

Logan arrived at the main house in record time. "Collin!" He strode down the dim hall with brisk purposeful strides.

"What is all that racket?" the old man complained from the dining room.

Logan marched in, snapping up window shades on his way.

With one eyebrow cocked, Collin eyed him from his place at the head of the twelve-foot table.

Logan yanked out a heavy chair. "Explain," he demanded, sitting down.

Collin lowered his soupspoon with overbearing slowness. "Explain?"

"This." Logan tossed Suzanna's letter across the table.

Collin glanced from the letter to Logan and back to the letter again. The edges of his expression quivered with the start of a smile. "Well, well." He sat back, the smile broadening. "I must say it's a pleasure to win one for a change."

Logan slammed the table with his fist, causing Collin's soup to slop over. "And just what have you won, Father? Tell me. I'd really like to know."

Collin wiped his mouth and calmly placed the napkin by his bowl. "Why, the boy, of course. That's what this contest with Suzanna Keating was all about, wasn't it?"

"No, Father. With you nothing is ever what it seems to be about."

Collin pushed to his feet, indignant. "Would you care to explain that remark?"

Logan thought about it. Maybe it was time someone forced Collin to look squarely at the root of his behavior. But then he let the urge go. What would be accomplished, aside from hurting the old man?

"What did you do to scare her away?" Logan asked, instead.

"I? I did nothing."

"What was it, Father? It couldn't have been money. Suzanna would never fall for a bribe as shallow as that."

"Oh, for pity's sake, leave it." Collin waved a hand and began to pace. "Can't you just be happy she's dropped the contest and gone? Now our lives can get back to normal."

Logan pressed his palms along his thighs, weighing his next words thoughtfully. "I have news for you, Collin. I don't have the slightest intention of letting Suzanna slip out of my life."

Collin's pacing stopped. "What do you mean?"

"I'm afraid another one of your sons has fallen for a Keating girl. I love Suzanna. Yes, I love her, and until a minute ago I didn't know what I was going to do about it. I was too busy trying to find a way to balance her and you and me, and keep everybody happy. But thank you, you just helped clarify my thoughts.''

Collin groped for his chair and reseated himself unsteadily. ''What are you saying, son?''

''Congratulate me, Father. I'm going to be married—if Suzanna will have me, that is.'' He watched Collin's color deepen, saw his shoulders lift, felt the fire of outrage building in his eyes.

''What did I do to deserve two such witless sons? You never ever marry a person you love. Haven't you learned anything in your thirty-two years? Didn't you see what happened to Harry? Love blinds. It clouds a man's judgment and ultimately becomes his undoing.''

This time Logan was unable to hold back the words. ''You would know, wouldn't you?''

Collin took the jab with a sharp intake of breath. ''Yes.'' He nodded. ''I know. That's why I can't bear to see you make the same mistake.'' He leaned forward, an arm reaching across the polished mahogany in supplication. ''Son, what you've got to do is find someone who's your equal, someone who you can be certain isn't marrying you to take advantage.''

Logan tapped the pads of his fingers on the table, fast, hard, faster. ''How many times do I have to say it? I don't love Cecily.''

''Good. If you don't love her, she can't lead you around on a leash. That's just the point I'm trying to make. People like us have to be rational when we approach marriage. Romantic love may be fine for the ordinary man on the street, but for us, no. It just gets in the way.''

Logan tried to believe Collin's only concern was his welfare, but he knew his father too well.

''I have a question.'' Logan folded his hands and very carefully placed them on the table. ''What if I don't take your advice? What if I continue to see Suzanna?''

Collin stared at him, a moment suspended in time. Slowly a smile curled over his dry lips, a smile that sent shivers down Logan's back.

CHAPTER TWELVE

SUZANNA AWOKE to an apartment that felt strange. It had only been two weeks since she'd slept here last, yet it no longer felt right. Somewhere else had come to feel like home, like the place where she wanted to wake up for the rest of her life.

Her apartment seemed doubly strange, she realized, because there was no puppy barking to be let out, no cartoon noises coming from the TV. It really wasn't her old place anymore.

Still, there were definite advantages. She dressed and ate without interruption, marveling at the ease with which she could go about her routine now that she didn't have a child to tend to. Her workday unfolded at a more leisurely pace, too, since she no longer had to cram eight hours' labor into four in order to fit in a visit to Mattashaum.

Yes, she was much better off now that she was alone and free of responsibility, she told herself a dozen times that day. She'd been caring for others for so long she almost didn't know how to live for herself. Maybe it was time she learned.

She didn't have a single doubt that Timmy would be better off, too. She truly believed the words she'd written in her letter to Logan. He would provide their nephew with the best of everything: an excellent education, a vibrant nurturing home and, even more importantly, character and values.

And then there was that not-so-small matter of Timmy's three million dollars. Her continuous loving care was a valuable asset, but compared to three million dollars, it paled. He would be able to do a lot with his life, given such an advantage. Furthermore, Logan's care was every bit as loving as her own.

It was Logan's welfare, however, that proved to be the centerpiece of the argument she was having with herself that day. With her out of his life, he'd eventually come into ownership of Mattashaum, as he should. He'd meet someone more suitable than she, someone he could love and marry and who had Collin's blessing, as well.

Without a doubt everyone was going to be better off.

But, oh, how she'd miss them! she thought, climbing the stairs to her quiet apartment at the end of the day. Would knowing she'd done the right thing ever take away this aching emptiness?

She entered the deepening gloom of her kitchen and opened a can of soup for supper. She tried to read the paper while she ate, but visions of Logan insisted on superimposing themselves on the print. She wondered what he was doing, what he was eating, saying, thinking, feeling. Was he wondering about her, too?

Probably not. More than a full day had elapsed since she'd left that note on his table, and he still hadn't called. It was clear that being free of her didn't bother him at all.

She was startled out of her bleak thoughts by a thumping on the side steps followed by the ringing of her doorbell. She frowned in curiosity, going to the window to see who her unexpected visitors were.

When she saw who was standing on the porch, a torrent of confused emotion surged through her.

"Come in." She waved Logan and Timmy in through the entry to her kitchen. Buddy scampered in, too, tail wagging in excitement.

"Hello, love," Suzanna murmured, giving Timmy a tight hug. Lord, she never wanted to let this sweet little boy go.

"Auntie Sue! You're squeezing." He giggled.

"Oh, I'm sorry." She released him, straightened and finally found the courage to face Logan. For several long seconds, they stared at each other. To Suzanna this day apart from him had seemed like a lifetime, and hard as she tried, she couldn't pull her gaze away.

Logan was dressed in pleated trousers and a shirt she suspected he'd ironed himself. He was freshly shaved but had nicked himself in three places, and his still-damp hair was mussed. Nevertheless he was the most appealing creature she'd ever seen, and she yearned to take him in her arms and never let go of him again, either.

Outwardly she didn't move a muscle. "Hi," she murmured, wondering why he was here.

He nodded back. "Mind if we visit awhile?"

"Not at all. Have a seat. Have you eaten?"

He shrugged. "We had a late lunch."

"I can bring something up from the shop," she offered. "Marie made an extra lasagna today."

Logan smiled a little, then a lot. "That sounds great."

Suzanna put away her unappetizing soup, and while her two favorite men set the table, she heated a hearty meal in the microwave. In short order, a bottle of wine had been opened and they were seated.

"So, what brings you here?" she asked. As if she didn't know. It was her letter. It was his gratitude for winning Timmy without a lengthy battle. It was maybe a discussion of visitation rights. She swallowed, hard.

"I have a favor to ask." Logan put down his fork and took a sip of wine.

Her curiosity stirred. "Go on."

"Do you have a spare apartment to rent?"

That was the last thing she expected to hear. "No. Why do you ask?"

"Well—" Logan cupped his chin on his palm, his face turned aside "—as of today, Tim and I are in need of a place to stay." He sounded nonchalant enough, but when he turned to meet her eyes, she saw the anguish he thought he was hiding.

The next moment it hit her—what he'd said, what he'd meant. She could scarcely draw a breath. They continued to stare at each other, frozen in the moment, eyes questioning, eyes confirming.

Logan was the first to break away. "We'll discuss it later, all right?"

She nodded, too stunned to speak.

Until Timmy was tucked to sleep in his familiar old race-car bed, Suzanna walked around on legs that wouldn't stop quivering. Did she dare believe she wasn't just caught in a dream?

When she and Logan were finally alone, seated on the sofa in the living room, she asked, "What happened?" And Logan spent the next half hour telling her. About finding her letter. About confronting Collin. About Collin's ultimatum. He told her everything.

"At first I was outraged that he'd stoop to such tactics with me. I'd seen him handle others that way, but I thought we were above that, that we understood one another, that we *loved* one another, for heaven's sake. But I guess you were right. He really is just a manipulative old man, obsessed with control."

"I'm sorry. I didn't want to be right. Honestly I didn't."

Logan refilled their wineglasses and settled back, resting his arm along the top of the sofa where it skimmed her shoulders. "After my initial anger wore off, I tried to reason with him. That's what I've always done—reasoned, mediated, kept the peace. I thought I could make him see his behavior objectively, you know, as a pattern that's resulted from being abandoned by people he's loved in the past—his father, his wife, Harris. I tried to sympathize, assure him that everyone needs to feel loved and he's no exception, but that he has to recognize he goes about it all wrong. He can't hang on to people with monetary threats and bribes."

Logan turned his head and lightly pressed his lips to Suzanna's hair, breathing deeply of its fragrance. She curled toward him, resting her arm on his chest, her fingertips lightly stroking his shirt where his heart beat.

"As tactfully as I could," Logan continued, "I tried to make him see the tragedy of being intractable. And that's the worst part. Once he takes a stand, he never gives an inch and causes a lot of unnecessary pain as a result. It's his damn stupid pride."

Logan raked his fingers through his hair. "I told him so, too, and by then I was too upset to pad my meaning with tactful phrases. I told him he could've saved his marriage if only he'd bent a little. He could've accepted Harris's marriage, too. Hell, we missed out on five of the best years of Harris's life. And why? Just because we couldn't say that maybe we were wrong."

Suzanna lifted her eyes to his. "We?"

"Yes, we. I have no excuse for not supporting Harry more, no excuse for not visiting and getting to know his wife. If she was anything like you..." The sentence went unfinished as he swallowed, then swallowed again. "I could have made their life so much more comfortable, Suzanna." His expression turned deeply pained. "And, Lord, how I wish I'd been around when Timmy was born."

Suzanna sat up, facing him. "Hey, what is this? Stop." She cradled his head in her hands. "It wasn't your fault. Collin started it. Harris could've been more cooperative, too."

But Logan shook his head, his eyes darkening with guilt and pain. "I did love him, you know."

Suzanna stroked the hair over his ears. "I know."

"He was such a bright personable kid. Always gave us fits with his harebrained ideas, of course...."

"I know that, too."

"But he had so much warmth, so much vitality."

"If it's any consolation, he never stopped admiring you, Logan. Or loving you," she added softly. "Oh, for a while he was angry, but later when he spoke about you, it was always with love."

"Thank you." His throat worked convulsively, Suzanna noticed. She brushed aside his hair and kissed his hot forehead.

"Getting back to Collin..." Suzanna sighed. "I gather he ignored most of what you said."

"Most? How about all?"

"I guess it's only natural. You reach a certain age and it must be hard to view your own behavior objectively, especially when it's being criticized."

Logan agreed. "And it's damn near impossible to change. Now I see he's as unbending with me as he's been with everyone else. And why?" Logan moved back, his mouth tightening. "Why has he driven off his only son and grandson? Because he needs an ironclad guarantee that he's loved, the old fool." He fell silent, his eyes fixed but unseeing. "That's what made my decision to leave so painful. Not that I'm losing Mattashaum, but because I love Collin, and the old fool doesn't even know it."

Suzanna grieved for Logan. She pulled him to her, linking her arms around his waist, and for several minutes they held each other, rocking gently, not saying anything.

After a while, when she sensed he felt better, she stood up and held out her hand. "How about a cup of coffee?"

"Sounds good." Logan followed her into the kitchen where she poured out two cups and handed him one.

"And now you're here," she said, leaning her hip against the counter. Filled with uncertainty, her eyes lifted to his and quickly dropped again.

"Yes, now I'm here." A smile teased the corner of his mouth. "Just as homeless as Harris was five years ago." He set down the cup, fit his hands around her waist and drew her to him. "And just as wildly and irrationally in love."

"In love?" She thought she said the words, though no sound came out.

Reading her lips, Logan nodded, his smile now glinting in his eyes. "Head over heels. In fact..." He hooked two fingers into his pants pocket and came up with a small blue velvet box. A ring box.

Suzanna stared in disbelief while he flipped open the lid to reveal a large diamond engagement ring. He started to remove it, but suddenly she slapped her hand over his. Even while her heart was soaring, she knew this wasn't what she wanted for him.

"I can't let you do this." She watched several emotions cross his face, not least of which was confusion. "You've got to go back home. I'm not worth what you and Timmy are giving up. Look at me. Look at this place. *Think,* for heaven's sake!"

"I have. I am." His eyes softened. "And I've never been more certain that what I'm doing is right." He stroked the back of his hand along her flushed cheek. "The only thing that gives meaning to life is love, Suzanna. You ought to know that. You're the one who taught me that lesson."

Logan removed the ring from the box, took a breath that lifted his broad shoulders and reached for her left hand. "I love you, Suzanna, and I can't imagine my life without you. Will you please do me the honor of agreeing to be my wife?"

Suzanna clutched his arm to steady herself. Marry him? Share his life forever? Her lips parted but she was too stunned to speak.

Taking her silence for reluctance, Logan rushed in with, "Before you answer, I want to assure you that, although I've lost Mattashaum, we're going to be just fine. Bradford Energy Systems is doing well. Going through the roof, actually." He smiled. "And over the years I've invested wisely."

"My catering business is growing, too." Suzanna cast him an accusatory smile, suspecting that he had steered a few new clients her way. "And we have a roof over our heads."

"See? We're going to do better than fine." Logan's eyes gleamed with love and hope while his voice grew uncertain. "So? What do you say?"

She shook her head in mock disparagement. "Do you really believe my answer depends on our finances?"

"Well, I . . . uh, no, but . . ."

"Yes," she said, dropping the answer into his embarrassed confusion like a two-ton boulder. The room went silent.

"What?"

"Yes. Okay." Suzanna's stomach bottomed out and she giggled with nervousness. "Let's do it."

"You mean it?"

She swallowed, feeling her eyes well up with tears. "With all my heart."

Logan expelled a deep breath in relief. With hands that shook visibly, he slipped the ring on her finger, then turned over her hand and kissed her palm.

"You've made me the happiest man alive," he whispered. A moment later she was in his embrace, kissing him with a fervor that matched his own.

Preparations for their wedding filled the next few days with joyful mayhem. It was to be a small affair, the five-o'clock ceremony held in the side chapel of Suzanna's neighborhood church, with a modest reception in the parish hall following the service. Marie, having married off three of her own daughters, was an old hand at organizing weddings and threw herself into the preparations with a gusto that left Logan reeling.

As for Timmy, he was so excited over the recent turn of events that he almost couldn't sleep.

"And we're always gonna live in the same house?" he asked several times each day. As often as he asked, it was still a pleasure to reassure him that, yes, indeed, they were now an indivisible family.

One evening two days before the ceremony, however, Suzanna looked up from the lacy bells she was filling with mints and tying up in tulle to see Logan frowning into space. The travel brochures he'd been reading lay forgotten on the coffee table.

"Logan?"

His head snapped up. "Mmm?"

She chewed the inside of her cheek. "Are you... having second thoughts?"

His brow tightened. Then, "Oh, Lord, no. Never."

"You looked so preoccupied just now."

He pressed his lips together. "Just thinking about my father and how nice it would be if he could share in our happiness."

Suzanna fingered the frilled netting of one of the completed favors. "I know. It's sad, isn't it? He's out at the beach all alone, and he isn't..." She ducked her head. There was no need to remind Logan that his father was old and unwell and wouldn't be around for long.

"Logan, I... um... sent him an invitation," she admitted into the soft cowl neckline of her sweater.

Logan's back straightened.

"I hope you're not upset. Oh, you are, aren't you?" And then she saw his grin. "What?" she asked suspiciously.

"I sent him an invitation, too."

"Oh. Oh, my."

They both laughed.

"But there's something else," she confessed, crossing the room to sit close beside the man whose generosity of spirit grew more apparent the longer she knew him. "I added a personal note."

Again he fixed her with his amused regard. "What did it say?" When she hesitated he added, "If you tell me about your note, I'll tell you about mine."

"You didn't! Oh, Logan." She pressed against him, laughing. "It wasn't much really, just a few words about love being like a light aimed at a mirror." She felt her cheeks warming. "This is embarrassing."

"No, go on."

"And, well, how the more love you project, the more you get back."

He nodded approvingly. "Mine was about oak trees. Oak trees and how they're the ones that usually go over in a hurricane because they won't bend. Poor Collin."

"Poor Collin," she agreed. "Between my mirrors and your oak trees, he isn't going to know *what* we're saying."

They shared a soft laugh, but Logan's amusement faded quickly, and soon he was frowning almost as deeply as before.

"It doesn't matter. He won't come. I talked a blue streak the day he and I had our argument, but nothing sank in. He certainly isn't going to pay attention to a couple of wedding invitations with cryptic messages scribbled on them."

Suzanna gripped Logan's two hands and, raising them, pressed her lips to his knuckles. "Maybe not today, maybe not next week or next month, but eventually we're going to solve this problem. We will. Together we can handle anything."

Logan pulled her against him. "You're incredible. Have I told you that yet today?"

She smiled, snuggling into the warmth of his neck. "I'm so happy, Logan." Then she whispered, "Sometimes I get scared it can't last."

His hand curved over the back of her head. "It'll last, I swear to you it will. This is only the beginning, my love." His mouth closed over hers, sealing the vow.

Somewhere on the edges of Suzanna's consciousness, a phone was ringing. The kitchen phone. Somewhere out there she also heard footsteps pattering across the kitchen floor. Reluctantly she pulled back from Logan's intoxicating kiss.

"Timmy got it," he murmured. The sensuous curve of his mouth told her he would like to continue what they were doing, but his imposed reserve warned that they were not alone.

"Hey, pal." He held out an arm and Timmy bounded across the living room and into his lap, followed by a tail-wagging puppy.

"You're getting to be such a big boy, answering the phone by yourself now!" Suzanna praised, stroking the child's pajama-clad arm. "You . . . didn't hang up, did you?"

"Nope." Timmy hooked an arm around Buddy's furry neck and settled himself and his dog more comfortably between his new parents.

"You told them you'd come get me?"

"Yup."

"Good boy!" Suzanna started to rise, but Logan held her back.

"I'll get it. You've been on your feet all day. By the way, Tim, did you ask who it is?"

"Yup."

Logan laughed at the teeth-pulling nature of their conversation. Therefore, he was more than a little surprised when Timmy went on to add, "It's Grandpa."

Logan glanced at Suzanna and noticed she looked as thunderstruck as he felt. The next moment they were both racing to the phone.

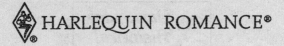

Harlequin® Historical

LOOK TO THE PAST FOR
FUTURE FUN AND EXCITEMENT!

The past the Harlequin Historical way, that is. 1994 is going to be a banner year for us, so here's a preview of what to expect:

* The continuation of our bigger book program, with titles such as *Across Time* by Nina Beaumont, *Defy the Eagle* by Lynn Bartlett and *Unicorn Bride* by Claire Delacroix.

* A 1994 March Madness promotion featuring four titles by promising new authors Gayle Wilson, Cheryl St. John, Madris Dupree and Emily French.

* Brand-new in-line series: DESTINY'S WOMEN by Merline Lovelace and HIGHLANDER by Ruth Langan; and new chapters in old favorites, such as the SPARHAWK saga by Miranda Jarrett and the WARRIOR series by Margaret Moore.

* *Promised Brides,* an exciting brand-new anthology with stories by Mary Jo Putney, Kristin James and Julie Tetel.

* Our perennial favorite, the Christmas anthology, this year featuring Patricia Gardner Evans, Kathleen Eagle, Elaine Barbieri and Margaret Moore.

Watch for these programs and titles wherever Harlequin Historicals are sold.

HARLEQUIN HISTORICALS...
A TOUCH OF MAGIC!

HHPROMO94

Where do you find hot Texas nights, smooth Texas charm and dangerously sexy cowboys?

Crystal Creek reverberates with the exciting rhythm of Texas. Each story features the rugged individuals who live and love in the Lone Star state.

"...Crystal Creek wonderfully evokes the hot days and steamy nights of a small Texas community...impossible to put down until the last page is turned."
—*Romantic Times*

"...a series that should hook any romance reader. Outstanding."
—*Rendezvous*

"Altogether, it couldn't be better."   —*Rendezvous*

Don't miss the next book in this exciting series.
SHAMELESS by SANDY STEEN

Available in July wherever Harlequin books are sold.

This July,
Harlequin and Silhouette
are proud to bring you

by Request™

CONVENIENTLY Yours

WANTED: Husband
POSITION: Temporary
TERMS: Negotiable—but must be willing to live in.

And falling in love is definitely not part of the contract!

Relive the romance....

Three complete novels by your favorite authors—in one special collection!

TO BUY A GROOM by Rita Clay Estrada
MEETING PLACE by Bobby Hutchinson
THE ARRANGEMENT by Sally Bradford

Available wherever
Harlequin and Silhouette books are sold.

HARLEQUIN® **Silhouette®**

Fifty red-blooded, white-hot, true-blue hunks
from every State in the Union!

Look for MEN MADE IN AMERICA! Written by some of
our most popular authors, these stories feature fifty of
the strongest, sexiest men, each from a different state in
the union!

Two titles available every other month at your favorite
retail outlet.

In May, look for:

KISS YESTERDAY GOODBYE by Leigh Michaels (Iowa)
A TIME TO KEEP by Curtiss Ann Matlock (Kansas)

In June, look for:

ONE PALE, FAWN GLOVE by Linda Shaw (Kentucky)
BAYOU MIDNIGHT by Emilie Richards (Louisiana)

You won't be able to resist MEN MADE IN AMERICA!

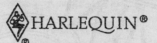